De

MW01592749

The Fire Warlock Series

BOOK 1

FOLEY

Written by Kate Benoit

Cover design and type editing by Debra Atwater.
Printed in the United States by Emporium Publishing Company

i

Introduction

Chapters

Introduction

Declan Patrick Foley born in 17th century Ireland; with jet black hair, piercing deep blue eyes and a captivating smile making him the "catch" of women's desires.

Declan lives between the worlds of darkness and light and roams it aimlessly searching for his only desire - Mary. The only woman he has ever loved or will ever love. A bond so strong that his blood cries out for her touch; he can feel her coming back to him, yet each time, she tragically leaves. He'll never give up; she is his only reason for existing in a world that will never end for him. You see, Warlocks don't die; but without his Mary, Declan has died inside a thousand times. He is lost and tortured without her by his side. He'll never give up because he will live forever and forever without Mary is a cruel joke that he can't allow to continue. He will keep trying to find her, to save her; until the end of time.

1

Summer Days

It is a bright, hot and hazy summer day in Connecticut, and I can't believe it's 2018! I also can't believe I'm back in Connecticut again. When the locator spell brought me here I thought, "Oh hell no, not again!" The last time I was here was 1938, in Milford; a coastal city in the southwestern part of the state, not too far from New York. Now, I'm in Guilford. A small town dotted with mystical shops, historic buildings, and stuck between two giant metropolitans; New York and Boston. Perhaps here I'll have better luck. I finally found a profession that I really like and it only took me a few centuries. I'm not just biding my time until I find her this time; I'm finally doing something for me and Mary, not just for Mary.

Like any other day, for the past 5 years, I got up, shut off the blaring alarm, showered, dressed, shaved and went into the kitchenette to make coffee. I can get something to eat at work. God knows they're always cooking something. As I grab the to-go mug off the shelf I think, "better make it black today, I need the caffeine." As I walk to work, I'm thinking of Mary and hoping tonight's the night I find her. The locket brought me here. I know she's here close by, I began to think as I strolled in about 15 minutes to 11 to start my shift at the firehouse. Working the 11-7 shift is a pain but once I find her I'll still have evenings to take her out and court her. When it gets serious, I can see about changing to mornings to have my nights with her. I sit waiting for the sirens to sound as I do each shift here. I was beginning to get bored looking at the same four concrete grey walls that sometimes get painted vivid blues or yellows by bored firemen or would-be artists trying their hand at a mural to brighten our environment. Inevitably, someone would tire of it and paint over it. Over time the walls went back to a muted grayish look. The only bright spot in "the house" as we called it was the kitchen where those with culinary skills brought in their spice racks, brightly colored pots & pans and where posters of Food Network stars glistened on our walls for inspiration. But, I can clearly see greasy handprints on the walls now and vow that my next project will be painting the joint!

I'm getting really hungry now and the aroma of food is calling to me. Paul, Tyler & Colin are eating in the kitchen; smells like burgers and fries again. Paul and Colin are brothers; and have been firemen for about a year. Both of them have absolutely no culinary skills! Burgers and fries are their signature dishes and they're usually well-done to almost burnt. They're only a year apart and they almost look like identical twins with their blond hair and blue eyes. Paul is taller at nearly 6′ 3″ while Colin is just about 5′ 11″ – "Tall Paul and Little Colin" are names tossed around by these jokester brothers. Tyler has been with the "house" the longest, two years more than me, and he's been a fireman for almost 5 years as he joined up at 19, right after high school. With his thick brown hair, pale green eyes and boyish grin, he looks like he's still in high school! He learned to cook out of necessity. He has spent long, endless hours at the station and became tired of the same routine of dogs, burgers and pasta. He picked up a few cookbooks and began trying out recipes and found he had a knack for it! The recipes became like science projects to him and we began calling him the "The Mad Chef" on days like today though, he lets the others cook for a change and really doesn't mind their food, as it gives him a break, though he is planning on making a chocolate cake with a caramel center later. He's been wanting to try out that recipe for a long time, and knows the guys will enjoy his effort, and hopefully the cake!

The kitchen is an eclectic place filled with a variety of dishware from all our homes, gifts sent to us by thankful people we've helped and even from local restaurant owners who occasionally send over trays of food for the guys on shift. We have one long, family-style table where there's always something to eat on it; from fresh fruit to old pizza, there's never a shortage of some kind of food. The other guys were watching a baseball game in the back of the lounge. The room has an old, brown leather couch and some recliners that had been donated by family members and even the town. I can't understand how grown men can get so pissed off over a team losing; Boston Red Sox are beating the NY Yankees again 10-2.

Too bad Jousting isn't still in style, I love to

Joust...now, that's fun! Maybe I should join the local fencing team as I am very good with a sword. I'd better be; my life could depend on it someday. I spend more time here than at my apartment. But, I know I'll find her soon, I can feel it in my bones and I can't shut it off; no matter what is happening. I feel her and the longing is becoming unbearable.

The hairs on the back of my neck start to twitch when she's near. It's like an adrenaline rush that reaches down into my soul and up through the nerve endings of my body causing the locket in my pocket to vibrate a pulse that only I can sense. It's been 25 years since the last time I saw her and I'm getting anxious for her touch, her smell – I need her! I know she's here in town somewhere and I have to find her. After I had my fill of burgers and fries I sat down to watch the game. As I start to fall asleep, almost like a daydream state, and I'm seeing her, kissing her and just holding her close to my heart, it's like she's truly with me and then…the alarm sounds! Sirens are blaring, they jolt me away from my love like a cruel game.

The guys and I run and jump into our pants, pull up our suspenders, grab our hats, jackets and boots and down the pole we go. We lunge onto the engine, Truck 173 is a 2006 Sutphen with a 100′ Tower Ladder, and I take shot gun.

As we hit the streets at top speed, the trees, stores and people dotting the area become a blur of colors, and within a few minutes I can smell the smoke. We pull up to a large burning brownstone that is 3 stories high with flames shooting out of the 2nd floor windows. The tenants are running out of the building, some are yelling, even screaming, and some have that glazed over look and stare in stony silence. An old man starts shouting that someone is still in the building on the 3rd floor and they are trapped. I have to think quickly I can't let anyone see me use magic. I must cast a spell first in order to become fireproof. I run in first which I always do so no one suspects anything. I can't let them see my eyes as I run up the stairs I start to chant:

"In times of dire, into the fire,

from cellar to roof, make me fire proof."

As I run into the burning building my eyes are searching each apartment as I go by and the flames are getting out of control. My thoughts are racing with the rapid beat of my heart, and I know I'd better find someone soon or they won't make it.

As I hit the third floor, the space is smaller and there's just one large apartment. Towards my left, I see the door open and a young woman with light brown hair lying on the floor barely breathing. She manages to whisper, "my baby, save my baby girl" as I quickly pick her up and run into the hall, handing her over to the Chief who got to the top of the stairs a few seconds behind me. "How did you get her out Dec?" He's yelling over the noise of the fire, the clamoring of ladders, hoses, and I scream back "Chief there's still a child in there; here, take her, I'm going back for the little girl." "NO" Chief Ryan screams. "That's an order, Lieutenant." I ignore him and run back into the burning apartment, to the back of the house past the living room and through the kitchen, Now, I hear a faint choking sound as the flames begin to grow even higher. I run to the back of the apartment down a short hallway searching the bedrooms, and finally I find her in a smoke filled pink nursery, flames roaring all around me now and even flickering up through the floor below but I can see her, she's in her crib, a beautiful little baby girl, not much over a year old, I guess. With blond ringlets and pink pajamas just lying in her crib; she's not choking now, she's not moving or crying at all. I rush to pick her up and whisper to the child:

> *"Flames and smoke will deflect*
> *as this wee babe I protect."*

9

Just then she starts to scream. Did she see my eyes? No, she's just upset and I'm a stranger in a mask. "Hush wee one, you're safe with me, Mommy sent me to get you and bring you to her. She's just downstairs waiting for you." "Let's go see Mommy" I say as I throw a blanket over her and rush her out of the room and down the stairs. There on the street near our Medic One truck is her Mother sobbing hysterically. "Ma'am, here's your baby," "Thank you, thank you" she says over and over, between sobs of joy and relief, as she clutches her child to her chest. "I can't believe you got to her in time, the fire was so bad and her door was hot, I tried but couldn't get to her. I thought I lost her forever." "No, it's my pleasure, just doing my job." "Maybe for the last time" Tyler whispers in my ear. I'll calm him down later and make up some kind of excuse like always.

Something about a small window of opportunity that I knew I could make it, something along those lines, maybe throw in that I used CPR on the baby to get her breathing. After all, I am the best fireman here, yes, I cheat but I save lives and that's what really matters. Well, I guess I've done this one too many times because when I get back to the firehouse there's a message for me in my mailbox to see the Chief.

After getting my ass handed to me on a silver platter, I go into the lounge where Colin is sitting, "Great, I'm on suspension again, now what?" "Two weeks with no pay that's what" Colin says with a laugh. "Dec, don't you ever learn? Ryan is the chief, what he says goes. He won't stand for that hero crap you pull all the time. You really did it this time; you could have not only killed yourself but that little baby too." "How many times do I have to say it, I'm sorry! I saw a chance and I took it. It all turned out for the best." "Guess I'll see you in 2 weeks." "Don't do anything I wouldn't do" Colin shouts as I leave. I chuckle to myself, if he only knew.

I'll take this time to hone up on my spells. That was too close today. I could have lost that child if I hadn't thought of something when I did, otherwise, it would have been too late. I made a promise to myself that no female would ever die in my arms again and especially not a baby. It's been years since I've been to Paris; maybe I should call a couple of my Warlock brothers and practice some really high tech magic. Declan laughed to himself and thought, "Warlocks ... we know we're Witches but Liam and Henry prefer the Old English and Scottish terms for males, so I humor them."

I'll see if Liam and Henry are free and what they've been up to these days, plus it will take my mind off of Mary, if that's even possible, as she dwells within my blood. I can't help but wonder what she'll be like this time, what she'll look like this time, even though none of that matters it's just fun to imagine... blonde, brunette or redhead?

Even though I do prefer red hair and green eyes.

Things are looking up! Liam and Henry agree to meet me in Paris, just what the doctor ordered! They know everything about the past and what I'm going through. It's good to have brothers to talk to and who listen; it's not like I can really talk to the other guys at work, as I can't be honest with them, and these centuries old friends have kept my sanity throughout the ages.

I met Liam when we were kids in Ireland when we were about 10 years old; he was playing out in the fields practicing his magic as I was strolling by. Liam was turning frogs into puppies and I started to laugh. "What's so funny, think you can do better?" "Yes" I said and turned the remaining frog into a tiger. We laughed as the tiger chased the dogs - until he started to chase us and Liam yelled "TURN HIM BACK STUPID!" "Oh yeah, I forgot I could do that" I said and turned him back to a frog. That day a brotherhood began.

It wasn't until Salem that I met Henry. He owned the local blacksmith shop and hired me on the spot. He said he liked the way I handled the horses; almost like I knew what they were thinking. I didn't find out for weeks that he was a Warlock too. I caught him one morning shoeing the horse with magic. "HEY" I said "no fair but I can do that too." Since that day we formed a brotherhood bond. I never imagined that Liam and Henry would become such good friends, seeing how completely different they are.

Henry hides his powers and Liam's a showoff. It's funny how the two of them hit it off and have remained friends since I introduced them: When I headed home to Ireland after Maggie died, Henry decided it was too hot to stay in Salem and left with me. That was the first time I had returned to Ireland since the day Mary died. Liam said things had changed so much after the Cromwellian conquest of Ireland in 1652 that he wasn't sure why he stayed but he was ready to move on, too. From that time on, Liam and Henry travelled the world together but I followed Mary's locket wherever it took me.

I thought about flying but decided against it and popped myself over to meet them. Paris was in bloom! I'd forgotten how the locals liked to put plants out on their balconies. Flowers were cascading over wrought iron fencing, large pots and even small trellises. Jesus, was it always so pink here? Mary would love it. "Hey brother it's been way too long, how the hell are you?" I could hear Henry's voice coming from down the street. Henry is a very muscular man, not too buff but you can definitely see he works out. He has Blue eyes, and is 6' 2 with sandy blond hair. He's dressed in jeans and a white t-shirt. His hair is a bit longer than I remember; must be something new to attract woman, not that he needs it. I can't remember a time that a girl said no to him. Next to him stands

Liam, whom women have said has emerald eyes, or so he says. His brown hair is short; he stands about 6' and is dressed in a suit and tie. All the women on the street look as they walk by. "What a pair you make." I say I as they walk towards me. "It's been way too long brothers, I really needed this vacation. But are we hanging out or going out? I can't tell by the way you two are dressed. Talk about night and day!" "Vacation, I thought you came to work?" Liam said. "We rented a place in the country for us to practice, out of sight so no one can accidentally see us casting spells." "Great! I need the practice because just last week I almost killed myself not thinking quick enough." As we get into our small talk like only good buddies can, Henry says "Hey Declan, do your eyes still shoot flames?" "No, you ass! They don't shoot flames they just have fire in them when I'm casting or using magic. You're just jealous because you can't do anything brilliant like that." "Yeah right, you're

16

brilliant, I forgot." We all laughed. It was good to joke around with them it's been so long.

We stopped at Café de Flore on the corner of the Boulevard Saint-Germain and the Rue St. Benoit for a drink and to talk for a bit. "It's getting late." Liam said, "We need to get going. I've rented a cabin in the woods deep in England so that we don't get disturbed." We drove his van through Paris, across the bridge to England while still reminiscing about the old days. The cabin was a mansion to me after my efficiency apartment, so much for my thoughts of it being a little log cabin! It was set back in the woods, back from the street view of the cars passing by as we drove down a steep and winding driveway to reach it; and there it stood in all its glory sitting on about 5 acres of land. It was rustic yet elegant looking with its well- maintained appearance. It had a front porch with a couple of rockers on it too, which gave it a warm, inviting look. The backyard had a fenced in pool area but the woods beyond it seemed to go on forever. "I rented the place for the month. There are plenty of rooms with a huge back yard, get settled Declan and come down in the morning and we'll start practicing at dawn." "Let's not waste time there's too much to do, so, why not start tonight?" I said as I walked into the living room. As I look around I knew it was Liam's magical handy work, He replaced everything with magic to suit his needs; the place was majestic inside! Fit for any royal vacation spot. White marbled floors with specks of gray were shiny and pristine looking throughout the first floor with scatterings of the finest looking oriental carpets adding warmth and color. Over-sized comfy looking chairs placed around a fieldstone fireplace with a fully stocked bar area was a perfect mans-cave, and just what I needed!

I went up to the 2nd floor and found my room. It had an antique, Victorian king-sized bed with lions on the blankets and sheets, he thinks he's funny. I zapped a nice black quilt and black satin sheets on the bed. I put my bag down and started a fire with a snap of my fingers. The fireplace was magnificent with a combination of marble and cobblestone for an interesting old and new world look. There was a brass grate in the front and golden brass pokers on the stand. With my own bath fit for any king; I quickly showered, threw on a pair of jeans, a t-shirt with Black Sabbath's name across it, and went back downstairs. "What's first? I'm ready!"

Out in the yard, beyond the pool and way back in the open field we stood in a circle and could feel our energy becoming one in brotherhood. Old magic, new magic entwining our thoughts and surging up through our very souls was a powerful feeling indeed! As the midnight hour approached, we practiced our "flaming swords" with a focused thought and an outstretched hand. It appears as if our very arms turn into swords that can produce straight lines of fire to detract any enemy. If they dared to come any closer they'd be met with a fatal blowtorch to their chest.

After 2 weeks of this, I may not want to go back to work! I could stay forever if I had Mary here, too. Alas, but the 2 weeks flew by and it was time to go back to the states, back to Guilford and back to find Mary.

2

Sarah Spencer

Born Aug. 25, 1994 in Branford, CT, Sarah Mary Spencer was a raven haired, green eyed beautiful tiny baby girl. Sarah was quickly growing into a very bright and intuitive child. She made excellent grades in school and found that history came easy to her. She loved reading old novels, however she loved the old TV reruns of Bewitched and I Dream of Jeannie more. She often dreamed about the world of magic but for some reason could not figure out why it fascinated her so much; anything with the occult did. She even had the proverbial black cat that she begged her parents for. It was her 8th birthday when she got Tabitha, the tiny orange kitten, as a gift from her grandmother. She even called Tabitha her "familiar" after she saw an old film called "Bell, Book and Candle". She spent hours talking to her cat and the rest of her time usually trying to push people away. Sarah spent many hours alone in her room, and once told her mother that she was very thankful she was an only child. She was glad not to have brothers or sisters to deal with even though there were times that Sarah secretly wondered what it would be like to have a sister, but quickly decided it should be a brother if at all. He wouldn't take her clothes, play with her dolls or share a room. Yes, a brother might be nice, even better a twin brother. She often felt that a part of her was missing; that she wasn't a whole person. The only thing she missed as a child was someone to confide in about all her theories and phobias; someone to just be in the same "boat" as her.

Sarah had phobias that she could not explain to anyone not even herself. She shook all over and trembled with every thunderstorm; once when she was 8, she hid under the bed and refused to go to school. It was just a rainy morning with thunder rolling in the distance with occasional glimmers of lightning flashing across the greyish sky; but to Sarah it was the end of the world. Her fear paralyzed her and she felt like the storm would never end, never pass, and somehow it would stop her world from going on. Her fear was thick as if she could touch it; she knew it was just a storm, yet with each flash of lightening she couldn't stop herself from shaking with a foreboding feeling that this was bad, really bad. Her mother tried everything, and finally said "Sarah it's just God bowling, the thunder can't hurt you." Sarah cried out, "It's what comes next...the lightning, and I'm not going to school today! Can't I just stay right under here with my flashlight and Tabitha?" Her mother said, "Alright, but just this once, you have to get over this fear, I don't know why you are so afraid."

She also had nightmares of drowning; one night she awoke full of sweat, gasping for air, it was so vivid. She was at the beach just lying on her towel, face down, when a boy ran by and hit her with a ball. She was covered in sand and decided to go swimming just to wash it off. It was hot and she was sweaty and with the sand sticking to her skin she couldn't stand it. She went out into the water, just over her head, as she could feel her toes no longer touching bottom, when all of a sudden a whirlpool grabbed her and pulled her under, try as she might, she couldn't get out! She thrashed about and down she went, trying not to gulp in water, but then she felt her body, her spirit, beginning to drift away and she felt for certain that she was drowning. Suddenly, she felt a rush inside of her and jolted awake; still feeling the ocean on her skin, but it was her own sweat that clung to her. She could still feel the whirling in the water, as if she had been inside a washing machine that went crazy and then tossed her out and pushed her towards shore. Her body was still reeling from the turbulent dream and she vowed never to go into the water again; she would never trust it; she just couldn't take that chance.

Her parents were worried at one point when she hit her teen years and only dressed in black; wore black t-shirts, black jeans, black sneakers, she even wore black bras, panties and socks. With her black hair she looked the part of a witch; all she needed was a broom. The other children were afraid of her, except for Joan Reynolds. They met the first day of high school and became fast friends. Sarah finally found someone to share her phobias, hopes and dreams with, but more important someone to go to the mall with.

Even as a teenager she never really wanted to have children, she never got along with them. Joan was much better with them and they really seemed to like her. If she and Joan would babysit, they always go to Joan but with Sarah they threw up on her, yes, she thought better to just have her cat. They don't answer you back. These things she was sure of although she didn't know why. One day she said to Joan, "Maybe, she said with a laugh, I was a pregnant cat who was frightened in a lightning storm and drowned in the river." Joan just smiled and said, "Oh Sarah, what an imagination you have." But in all reality. she didn't know how close to the truth she really was. But what she was sure of was that one day she would find her Prince Charming; he would ride up on his white horse to come save and protect her forever and ever - they would live happily ever after.

Oh, how she wished that. Joan only dreamt of going to culinary school in France. As with all childhood fantasies; this phase ended just before graduation. She didn't need a man to make her happy; she had dated often but found that there was no spark, no passion, no fire when they kissed her, held her hand or even when she looked into their eyes; she saw and felt nothing: No twinkle and definitely no fire! It was like she was kissing a dead body she thought. Why am I so cursed? She thought, maybe there's something wrong with me. She wasn't going to settle for just any boy, she wanted it all. She wanted to feel her heart pounding in her throat. She wanted the cold clammy hands, sweaty palms and the tingle in her stomach.

She wanted to gaze into his blue eyes, she decided right then and there they had to be blue and he had to have black hair. He had to love her beyond words; and she wanted to hear his voice as he spoke her name, "Sarah, my love." Yes, that's exactly what I want she thought.

Before starting college, Sarah decided it was time to travel. She always wanted to see Europe, especially Italy. She had a few years of Italian in school and couldn't wait to test it out. She felt strangely more comfortable thinking about going to Europe than she did visiting other states. After all, Joan would be in Paris and maybe they could find a weekend here and there to see each other. She hated the thought of not seeing her for 4 years. Sarah's parents had saved up enough money for her to buy a used car but she decided to take that trip to Europe instead. A trip of a lifetime she thought, and she'd figure out how to get around without a car later on. But, right now, she wanted to venture out on her own and see some of the world! Her parents weren't supportive at first, feeling she shouldn't be traveling on her own in a strange country, but, they also applauded her courage of breaking out of her comfort zone. Plus, she was considered an adult now, so they decided to back off and let her fly! Saying goodbye to Joan was very hard, "I'll miss you Joanie, don't forget to call. I'll text you when I get to Italy and you text when you get to France." Joan began to cry, "Why are we doing this? Can't you come to France too?" "No, Joanie you want to be a pastry chef and I haven't a clue yet. I'd just hold you back. Plus, just think of all the gossip we'll have now. *"il mio più caro amico addio!"* "Au revoir, mes amis!" Joan said with a laugh.

Sarah had a swift flight and soon she found herself in a water taxi in Venice. She even got to see and brush the hand of the Pope in Rome during his Papal Audience time. She traveled along the countryside meeting friendly locals, who were always inviting her in for some food and wine. She loved exercising her high school Italian, although, the dialects were very different from region to region. She took tons of photos to share with Joan when they meet up next month. They decided to try to see each other at least twice a year. One a year Sarah would go to France and once a year

Joan would come to Venice. They had to limit girl talk to once a month but could text almost daily.

Before leaving for Europe, Sarah had read a book on how to travel "on-a-dime", and she did just that! She rented rooms here and there for very little money in homes of people with signs in their windows inviting tourists to stay with them. That was about it, just a room, with a bed and a dresser and everyone shared the bathroom, but she didn't mind. This could be a once in a lifetime journey and she was up for the challenge and the adventure!

While there, she decided it was time for a change, so she dyed her hair red and began to dress more like a lady. No black hair for her, no black hair or clothes. She'd always wanted to go red. She felt she was born to be a redhead. Sarah began studying books and voraciously absorbing all literature on ancient times. She loved the people, the language and the country so much she began leading tours in Italy and to sacred sites throughout the Mediterranean countryside and sea. Here she discovered the Tarot. She found that she had a real talent for reading the cards; it came to her like second nature. It was fitting that this happened while she was there, as Tarot card reading originated in Northern Italy during the early 15th century. She was an intuitive reader, she saw things in them that no one else did, and it was uncanny. She read for the people who rented her a room, her new friends and even shop owners, and they were shocked at how accurate she was. No matter who it was, a friend or a stranger, she was always right. It freaked people out but not her; the more she read the more she wanted to do it again.

Once, during a reading she pulled the death card and the woman she was reading for began to have a panic attack. "Not to worry!" she said,

"You're not going to die but I'm afraid that an ending of some kind is coming, could be a job or a relationship." The next day the woman came in and said her husband had left her. Things like this happened often, with quick and precise accuracy.

Sarah missed her family back in the states and while she had kept in touch with them almost daily for the past few years, she knew it was time to return. She had lived and learned all that she was meant to while in Italy, but now that she just turned 23, she felt it was time to go back home, back to the states and really start her life as an adult woman. Joan was finishing up in France and coming home, too. She couldn't wait to see her. Plans had fallen through so many times and they never got to see each other in person over the years.

Sarah ended up in Guilford, only because she wanted to be close to home but at least a town away. With all the money she made as a tour guide, reading cards, and newly accessible trust fund her grandmother left her she decided to open up a shop in Strawberry Hills. It was a quaint group of small stores and upscale boutiques, which sat right off the main road. She'd sell magical things like crystal balls, mystical things like pendulums, and she would read the Tarot cards, runes and palms in the back. Everyone thought she had lost her mind but she made her dream a reality. She hired Joan to work in the evenings to help around the store and to stay with the register while she did her readings. Joan had become a pastry chef and was trying to save money to open her own bakery. Although Sarah had made money in Italy, Joan had been studying and learning, if she wanted a bakery someday she would have to work her butt off for it.

She worked in a bakery during the day and at the store during the evenings. As Joan walked in, she looked around at all the work Sarah had done in such a short time, she said, "Sarah, I love what you've done with the place it's enchanting, and smells marvelous!" The shop was very bright and had a calming effect as you walked in the door. Incense burned to give the mystical smell, though it was not overpowering, just a light fragrance that seemed to enhance one's energy. Crystals hung from the ceiling in different sizes, shapes and colors, and they sparkled from the sun's light and twinkled rainbow effects throughout the store. She had quite a collection of jewelry that she had brought back from Europe; mostly pewter. She had a large selection of different Tarot decks, a section on books about magic, crystals, astrology and different sizes, shapes and colors of polished stones. There was a small table and chair set up for customers who wanted to sit and look at a book before buying. There was a sign on the counter that read, "Tarot readings $1 a minute".

In the first year, things were going great, the business was thriving. Friends and neighbors came to purchase things and for reading too; it was like one of her dreams were coming true. Until the readings started to become all too true, every time, exactly as she told them. People started to question where she was getting her information from. One day, one of her customers, Amy Santiago, burst into the back while she was performing a reading, "You BITCH!" "Thanks to you my boyfriend left me!" My client started to get up. "No! Don't go, I'll be right back. Amy let's take this to the front." "What happened and why are you blaming me?" "You said there was another woman in his life when you read my cards and I confronted him and he admitted to cheating on me and said he was glad I knew and left." "Wait, I didn't say that; you completely misunderstood. I said it could have been his mother or his sister I never said girlfriend." "I said it was the Queen of Pentacles and a nurturing woman, it could have been you I was seeing. You can't blame me for that." Amy turned in a huff and stormed out yelling to anyone who would listen that I was a witch casting spells.

It wasn't long after that people stopped coming. Then it happened; her first threatening note, as her hand began to tremble, she opened the folded paper and began to cry as she read the words:

"WITCH, LEAVE TOWN AND GET OUT WHILE YOU STILL CAN! YOU'RE NOT WELCOME HERE ANYMORE!"

At first she thought it was one of the bratty Benson boys, who always walked past the store on their way home from school usually making loud remarks about the store being haunted due to what I sold, and I thought they were just playing a prank. That night, she was at home when the police called to inform her that the alarm was going off in the store. Sarah rushed to the store to find a huge rock had been thrown in the window and smashed the front display case. Broken crystals everywhere, the rock had a note taped to it that said, *"You've been warned!"*

"What the hell is going on," she said to the Officer, "Am I living in Salem back during the witch trials being accused of witchcraft? This is insane – it's 2018, isn't it?" "Sorry Ma'am but people don't like this kind of voodoo around here." said Officer Abbott, "I'll look into it but I don't think we'll catch the culprits." Sarah said with a laugh, "I'm sure you'll add my file to the bottom of the case load. No hurry, it's just my livelihood!" A few days later after putting things back to normal Sarah decided to stay late to go over the books after Joan had left. She needed to see just how much this was going to set her back. Things were getting bad and she knew she had to cut Joan's hours to a couple of nights a week instead of the five she had been working. Poor Joan, she had been so loyal to her and she knew she needed this job too, so she would try to give her as many hours as she could until she was back on her feet. She began to nod off when a loud crash from the front of the store startled her. She went to see what was going on when she touched the door it was hot, very hot.

The store was on fire and she was trapped in the back. She chanted to herself, "DON'T PANIC, DON'T PANIC," "think Sarah," as she grabbed her cell phone to dial 911, only to notice that she had no signal. "SHIT! Now what?" There were no windows in this room, she was trapped. I'm going to die, just like a witch burned at the stake, was all she could think. She froze and her life started to run through her mind. I can't die yet I haven't had sex yet. This is what I get for waiting for Mr. Right.

3

Saving Sarah

Back to work, 11-7 graveyard shift again. I guess I deserved that. I did enjoy the time with the guys. Just hanging out and casting spells like the old days. I have a lot of new potions to try out. The smellier they are the more powerful they are...just the way it seems to work! I also love blowing things up, it's a guy thing and I can't very well do too much of that here in the States. Alarm rings - it's 9:00 p.m. already. I have a strange feeling, a good one, not just about the time I had in England, but I think I'm closing in on finding Mary. Feeling really anxious tonight, my hands are shaking, my knees are weary and I feel sick to my stomach. Something is going to happen; I'm sure of it. I always fear she won't fall in love with me this time. I can't think that way; I know she always does, every time it's the same thing over and over; she always falls in love with me again so I don't know why I worry about it so much.

I decided to walk again tonight. The night air has the pleasant scent of Yarrow, a hearty flowering bush that blooms this time of year, and it only makes me more melancholy for the sweet scent of my Mary. She's an ache inside of me that is never put to rest till I hold her in my arms. Most of the stores are closed except for a bar and a coffee house and now I see the lights from the firehouse as I round the corner. Oh, no sweet odors there! It's the aroma of sweat, metal and strange foods depending on who was cooking that night. As I approach the firehouse it's just about 10:45 pm. It's become a home away from home. The lights are always on; someone is always there. Somehow I find that comforting. My foot is barely in the door when the alarms sound off and we're off to a fire on the Post Road. What a way to start back! I just walked through the heart of town where everything was pretty quiet except for some loud laughter at Casey's Bar & Grill. So, what the hell happened and where? It must be arson, I thought. As we rush to the scene, it's on one of the main streets just on the edge of the town's center; we see that it's a small shop with a sign that reads "Tarot Readings by Sarah."

In the back Sarah saw the smoke coming under the door when she heard the fire trucks coming just before she started to pass out. We start to smash in the front window and notice there's someone in there. I know better this time - do not try to play hero! "There's a light in the back, someone must still be in there; it must be the owner!" I yelled out. "We'll cover you" I hear Tyler yelling. As we rush in, Tyler starts to douse the flames, they were growing, the flames were everywhere and beginning to surround the shop. As I was running to the back of the store I saw a closed door and immediately yanked it open; it was filling with smoke, but no fire in there yet. I can see a woman, with her head down, unconscious at her desk. Her hair is red as the fire, her skin a white as milk. She's very slender and petite. As I pick her up, a sensation runs through my body, the locket begins to throb in my pocket, my heart is pounding in my ears, I start to sweat, she's so still, I start to panic. Can it be, I think, is this Mary? She was in and out of it; she felt as though she was dreaming, did a man just bust down the door and pick me up in his arms? Prince Charming is that you? She thought, as she felt a twinge surge through her body as he held her close to his chest and carried her out. Smoke was burning and filling her lungs as she found herself losing consciousness again. Declan was drenched with sweat from the heat of the fire, the adrenaline rush and the thought of this woman being his Mary. "I can't be sure until she opens her eyes but I feel it; I can feel the tingling from my fingertips through the thick gloves and even in this heavy suit I feel the warmth of her heart, it's beating very slowly. "OH MARY, IS IT YOU? Have I finally found you again?" I murmur in her ear as I run faster than I have ever run in my life, out of the burning building to the ambulance that I hear roaring down the street.

There are so many people, why do people come out to see a disaster? Are they looking to see a dead body or get shot? So many thoughts running through my mind! There's too many people here and they're staring at me holding this woman, I can't risk getting caught using magic. I can't lose her before I even get the chance for her to open those beautiful green eyes. I know it's her, my Mary; it has to be the locket is never wrong. I can't feel this way for anyone else. My heart is pounding so loudly in my ears I can barely hear. No, wait the sign said Tarot Readings by Sarah; her name is Sarah this time. "Sarah, Sarah, can you hear me? I'm Declan, a fireman here to save you You're safe Sarah, you're safe, I've got you. Can you open your eyes for me? Please say something Sarah, I need to know if you are ok!" The EMT's are on the scene are trying to take her, I have to let her go, and she'll be fine. I'm right here. I can't look so concerned, someone will notice how freaked out I am over someone I'm not even supposed to know.

The EMT's are giving her oxygen now; she looks so helpless with the mask over her face. She's choking now that's a good sign. "She's taken in a lot of smoke, and we're taking her to Yale New Haven Hospital." The paramedic says. I have to step back and let them take her, it's so hard and then I hear Tyler saying we got it all but the front of the shop is toast. We were able to save the back, good thing she kept the door closed so it was contained to just the front of her store. As Tyler looked over at me I could hear him say, "Declan are you ok? Man, you look like you've seen a ghost." If he only knew how right he really was.

After my shift was over I popped over to the hospital to check on Sarah and to see if she was really Mary. I'd better turn invisible; don't want to scare the poor girl to death if it's not her. I'm in a hurry something very simple: *"I'm feeling invincible, make me invisible"* as the fire rises in my eyes I am totally see-through. I glide through the doors of the hospital ER like an invisible wisp; how free it felt to be in this state where no eye contact was made, no expectations or judgments – just me. The crisp white hospital corridors were humming with sounds of people talking and machines beeping. I was easily able to find the list of new admissions; it's amazing what transparent hands can uncover, and there was only one Sarah listed, Sarah Spencer. The chart is marked room

506. As I dodge people who can't see me, making sure not to touch them, I finally find room 506. I glide into the room, she's awake and there they are, those sparkling green eyes I've missed for the last 25 years. **I've found her, I knew it!** Look at her, I can't take my eyes off her, she's so beautiful, and I started to laugh. My Mary was as feisty as ever. She may not look the same but she still has that fiery spirit and she's still has those beautiful green eyes! The pale green room enhanced her striking green eyes even more against her delicate, porcelain skin and dark red, thick hair. She is breathtaking. Definitely taking *my* breath away!

At least I was able to pay for a private room for her anonymously. It was a small room with one bed, white sheets and a tan bedspread. The curtains were tan too, as was the tiled floor. Good lord it's so drab in here. I guess when you're sick it doesn't really matter but a little color would do wonders. I'll send flowers, roses in every color they make.

"Nurse! Nurse! I want to see a doctor, where are my clothes, I have to get out of here, see my store, what's left of my store, NURSE!" "Calm down sweetie, I'm right here." Nurse Snedeker said. There stood a woman about 5' 10" around 250 lbs. with black hair and hazel eyes, a stethoscope around her neck, cat print scrubs and white shoes. "You're not leaving until a doctor signs off on your case. Your chart says that you took in a lot of smoke last night. They kept the oxygen on you all night. I heard from the other nurses on duty last night that if it wasn't for some handsome fireman who rescued you, you may not have made it. In case you're interested, he stopped by and he's called several times to check on you to see how you are doing." Nurse Snedeker said. "Oh please, he's just probably worried I'll sue him." Sarah spewed. "My ribs are killing me, maybe he cracked a rib?" "Now don't be that way Ms. Spencer, you're never going to find a nice man that way. You could do worse than a handsome fireman." "HA, I don't need a man to make me happy; I do just fine on my own." Sarah spewed. Oh GREAT, she's not going to be that easy this time, she must be a women's lib kind of girl, oh no, please not one of those! I really do appreciate a strong woman, but I'm also old-school and like to open doors and pull out chairs – especially for the woman I love; it's more out of respect than anything else. I adore this woman. I have a feeling it's not going to be that easy this time. Just once I wish she was one of those women who want to find a nice man and settle down, have a few kids, a nice house with a picket fence and make it easy for me, but I guess that's just Mary's soul speaking. It's funny, she may look different each time and have a different name but it absolutely amazes me how her personality is so much the same as my Mary, a spunky lass!

Just then a blonde woman in a white chef's

jacket comes bursting through the doors, "Sarah, are you ok? I'm so sorry I left you alone last night." Joan said as tears streamed down her face. "I'm fine Joanie don't worry about me, what are you doing here? I told you I was fine and you should be at work." Sarah said. "I told them I had an emergency. I couldn't get any work done until I knew you were ok." Just as Joan finished speaking 2 police officers walk in the room. Both men were dressed in blue uniforms, black shoes, guns in holsters and badges. One had black hair and the other blond. "Ms. Spencer, I'm Officer Wayne Jones and this is my partner Officer Mark Smith. We have a few questions about the fire last night. Would you excuse us Ma'am?" "She can stay" Sarah replied. The officer continued, "The report is in and it was arson. Do you know anyone who would want to try to burn your store to the ground or hurt you?" "It could be any one of those crazy townspeople!" Sarah replied as Joan shook her head in agreement. "You see I have special talents if you will. I'm a Tarot reader, one of my many spiritual gifts and can I help it if I'm damn good at it. It's just a shame those damn idiots in town are afraid of me. I scare them. I've read cards for most of them and when I am correct or tell them something about their future and it comes true, they started calling me a witch. I feel like I'm in Salem," she laughs. "That's why when they started with threats and that didn't work they tried to burn me out. I've received several threatening letters saying leave while you still can."

Officer Jones spoke as he tried not to laugh. "Ms. Spencer do you have any of those letters that you can show us? Any proof as to what you are saying? These are strong accusations you're making and we just can't take your word for it." "I'm sure they all burned in the fire, how is my store?" "I'm sorry to inform you Ms. Spencer but the front of your store was heavily damaged; most of your inventory was destroyed, the owner of the complex will need to file a report with us and his insurance company; but right now, we need to board it up as it's not safe. Mostly just the inventory and furniture in the front is destroyed, what the fire didn't get the water pretty much damaged the rest, however, the back room managed to survive since you had the door closed. If you have renter's insurance, you should be ok."

"Well then, I guess all of the evidence is destroyed too, how convenient."

As I slip out of the room, I'm thinking better wait until later when she's had time to cool down and her friend has gone home. I'll come back just before visiting hours are over around 7 and see if she's in a better mood. Then, I can offer her a shoulder to cry on, yes, that's my way in, console her, and let her lean on me. I should offer to help her clean up the place, maybe ask Paul & Colin to help and say it's the firemen's way of lending a helping hand to the victims of arson, something along those lines. Yes, this could be a way to get closer.

Later that evening I stopped at a florist shop and picked up a bouquet of 12 long stemmed roses and ordered a dozen of white and yellow to be delivered tomorrow, and went to visit Sarah. She was watching a program on TV when I stepped into the room. "Ms. Spencer, I said." "Hi, I'm Lt. Declan Foley, the fireman who pulled you from the burning store. I just wanted to check on you to make sure you were ok. I know how drab hospitals can be so I brought you some roses to cheer you up." As she looked at them she glared at me. "Do you always check up on all of the people you rescue toting flowers?" "Must get expensive?" "No, no I just felt sorry that your shop's fire damage was so bad and wanted to check in on you, that's all" Boy she really isn't going to make this easy.

"I'm fine as you can see and thank you but I'm allergic to flowers you can take them with you when you leave." "And thanks to you. I think my ribs are cracked." "Sorry, I'm so sorry I didn't know, I'll bring them to the children's ward." Now, I sound like a babbling idiot, calm down and try this again. "Let me start over, I just wanted to see how you were that's all." "Thanks but I'll live. Don't you have a fire to put out somewhere? My boyfriend will be here soon and he won't be happy you stopped by." A BOYFRIEND, she has a boyfriend really? This time I have to get rid of a boyfriend? I just can't get a break, can I? "Sorry to have bothered you Ms. Spencer." As he started to leave she called him back, "Wait, wait a minute. I'm sorry too it's been a very long day and I've not only lost my inventory but it seems that I've lost my manners too. I just said that to get you to leave. Thank you for coming but it really wasn't necessary."

PHEW, I thought to myself. I dodged a bullet that time. This isn't going to be easy, no sir, not easy at all. I better call the florist first thing in the morning and cancel those other flowers. I better give her a few days and accidently run into her on the street. Maybe that kind of setting will work better. I'll try to fix Tyler up with that friend of hers Joan and maybe a double date would do. I started to think of how my journey all began back to my childhood and with my one true love, Mary.

4

<u>Mary Griffin</u>

I remember my childhood very well. It was when I met Mary and my life would be forever changed. In County Galway Ireland in the early 1600's, my family had a farm on about 20 acres and there was work going on from dusk to dawn. It was a hard life back then but simple compared to things now. Our house was small, a log cabin built by my father and his brothers; we also had a large barn where we kept a variety of animals; horses, cows, pigs, cats and there were always plenty of mice for them to toy with I'm sure. It provided a musical bed of animal noises from whinnies to cooing from the barn owls all day and night.

Chicken coops were outside the barn area providing fresh eggs to sell and eat. We also had this smaller cabin, more of a tiny ranch-hand house, where we could kick off our muddy boots during the rainy season or pour cold water over our heads during summer and not mess up our home; especially the kitchen where my mother would have a fit if we did that. But, that little cabin was magical too!

Growing up a Warlock was fun; when not working or going over our lessons, my mother used to teach us how to act in front of the mortals and my dad would teach us spells in that small cabin. So, if we broke anything, mother would not be upset. I had 3 sisters; Orla, Shannon and Maeve. I was a much faster learner than my sisters. Once I even turned Megan into a toad. I was given a punishment and had to chop all the wood for the fireplace for a week but it was well worth it to watch her hopping on the ground and eating bugs.

To this day when I see her I say "hey Meg had any good flies lately?" Funny, she doesn't find that amusing at all - she's a poor loser! I never held it against her or even got mad when she turned *me* into a rat and then turned herself into a cat and chased me all over the farm trying to kill me. Mother used to homeschool us even though there wasn't a name for it way back when. She was afraid we'd use magic in front of the other kids if we were around them too much or turn them into something if we got really mad. Since there wasn't an actual school in town yet and the others had to go to someone's house where a mom or older sister would teach lessons from old books; that could be quite awkward if one kid suddenly turned into a bird!

We were a tight-knit family, mostly staying to ourselves, but I did love Sundays as I got to play with other kids outside the church before and after services. My best friend was Joseph Riley Griffin.

He had a little sister Mary by about 1 minute; she was his twin. I thought that was funny because they weren't the same sex. She was a pest and would bother us when we were skipping rocks. I'm glad I don't have a twin…can't imagine two of me and I bet my mother can't either!

When I was 10 a schoolmarm moved into town and opened up the first schoolhouse in the area. It wasn't much bigger than our ranch-cabin on our property. The wood was painted red with 2 windows in the front. A one floor building with 10 wooden desks and a black slate board hanging on the wall. There was a small backyard with ropes hanging from a large, sprawling tree with boards attached to them so we could sit and swing; along with painted wheel barrels to cart each other around for fun. I remember the day mother said we had to start to mingle with other kids and that we needed to start to go to school so that people didn't start to talk. All the kids that were at church were there, and I was happy to see Joseph but then here comes Mary, too. I usually had to take my sisters along. At least at recess the girls went off to swing and talk and not bother the boys. Joseph and I walked and talked about knocking them off the swings but one of the other boys, that sissy William, wanted to tell on us. The good old days were fun.

About 4 years later the church was having something they called a *social* and we all had to dress up and go. Mother said there would be music, dancing and food. I don't want to dance with a girl, but I do want to eat. I don't even like girls they are too giggly and they scream around frogs and insects. I'd like to turn them into frogs but father said someday that would change. Dressed in my best Sunday clothes we hitched the horses up to the wagon and along we went. When we arrived at the Anglican Church we all went to, they had a larger room towards the back called the hall of communication where all parties of some sort were held. Just a large empty room really; the women from the church would decorate it for all the events to give it a festive look.

This time they decorated it with fresh flowers and multi-colored ribbons and there was music, which was a nice diversion from only hearing preaching on these grounds. The melodious sounds of the harpsichord and the lute put everyone in a good mood despite the stuffiness of the room, which had very little ventilation. I was getting bored and looking to get into trouble when she walked in. Mary Elizabeth Griffin: She was dressed in a blue dress, her red hair held a white comb with pearls, she had white gloves and white shoes; she was stunning. This was the first time I really saw her. What the heck was going on? I actually went up to her, like I was in a dream, and asked her to dance and she said yes!

Joseph wasn't happy but he danced with Shannon and I saw them having fun. Boy things were changing now! I would never look at her like Joseph's bratty little sister again. I started thinking maybe girls can be fun! We had a wonderful time. We danced all evening and I dreaded the end of each dance as I was afraid someone would cut in.

She felt so soft in my arms and she smelled so good. What was happening to me? I actually smelled her hair for God's sake. I felt my heart skip a beat when she smiled at me. I started to feel very warm all over, a tingle in my stomach all the way down to my toes. I couldn't stop smiling. If I didn't know better, I'd swear I was bewitched. Before I thought about it I cast a spell and held out my hand to her with a locket. "Here this is for you, Mary. I want you to wear it always." "I hope you like it, I inscribed something on the back." As she reached out to take the locket I could see that her eyes begin to fill with tears. As she opened the locket she could see inside, a tiny picture painted of him on one side and the Claddagh symbol on the other side. "Oh Declan it's beautiful. As she turned it over she read, "I love you more" with tears streaming down her cheeks she said, "I'll never take if off". That was the first of many happy memories.

Over the next 2 years we had a really great and beautiful courtship. We used to walk through the fields hand in hand and I would try to steal a kiss. To be a teenager in love again! I would tell her I loved her and she would tease and say "I love you more" as she placed her hand over her locket. Not true, no one could ever have loved anyone more than the way I loved her. Her kisses were so wonderful; her lips were so soft and warm. I couldn't believe I could be this happy. She was what my mother called a "Good Soul." All I could think about was asking her to marry me. It's the only way I wouldn't lose her. It would kill me if she left me or fell in love with someone else: I couldn't bare it. I want to have many children with her and I want a long, joyous life with her. I'll deal with the rest when the time comes. She was such a good person and good listener. We talked about almost everything from our beliefs to our dreams, but I was keeping a huge secret from her. I wasn't being entirely honest with her because I was forbidden to tell her I was a Warlock. I loved to play tricks on her and I would tell her to close her eyes, and with a little magic, a bouquet of roses appeared and she would open her eyes in surprise.

That was about it, my parents always warned me about the Witches Council and how they would take our powers away if the humans ever caught us or worse kill the human so that the secret would be kept safe from mankind. Our kind had to blend in, or we would lose it all, a code that had to be kept. It was always drilled into my brain that the humans just couldn't understand it. They would try to destroy us. Humans always feared the unknown. I couldn't risk Mary getting killed by the Council, but, I thought what if we were married then she'd have to know, right? I knew I had to go to her father and ask for her hand in marriage but first I better talk to my own parents.

My Father was furious with me. He slammed his fist down on the table and shouted, "You will not marry a human. You will marry a lovely witch that we have selected for you to marry next year. Her name is Maeve O'Brien and she comes from County Kerry. Her father and I have known each other for centuries and made a pact that our first born children would marry. You've met her before, she's lovely and it's settled." "OH NO, Dad not her, she's horrible and she's not Mary!" "Declan Patrick Foley, I will not discuss this with you any further, you will marry Maeve and that's final. The Council has already approved this union. They would NEVER allow you to marry a human. You know that the first rule is secrecy. It's the only way we can survive, Declan, you know this." While his voice was angry, his eyes looked sympathetic at me too, I could tell he was sad for me. "You say you love Mary? Do you want the Council to kill her? That's what will happen if you don't stop this foolishness." "Why does it have to be that way; can't we turn her into a witch?" "You have to be born a witch or kill one. Would you have her kill one of us so that you could have her?" He shouted and my mother started to cry. "Don't be like this, I love her and I want to marry her." "Instead of telling me why I can't, why can't you help me find a way?" "Declan, son, I love you and if there were a way I would do it, but a life with Mary only means her death." "The Witches Council can't be that heartless. She won't tell anyone. I know she won't." "Son," his mother said softly, "she wouldn't do it on purpose but it would come out and as she spoke the words she would die, is this what you wish for her?"

Heartbroken I ran to my room, which was only a few yards away from where my parents stood, so I could hear them speaking in low, soft tones. I dropped onto the bed and buried my face in my soft, feathery pillow trying to think of a way out of this and into a life with my Mary. We'll elope! That's it! We'll run so far away they'll never find us. I'll make a cloaking spell to hide us for as long as it takes. I'll keep her safe. I won't marry Maeve and no one can make me. I'll come back someday but for now I have to convince Mary to run away with me. What can I say to make her go? I can't spell her to go that would draw the Council's attention. I know she'll come away with me.

The Witches Council; my parents used to tell us stories about them. They were from the 8th century. They were created because a witch had spelled a man to love her. His fiancé at the time knew witchcraft was involved and learned how to kill a witch. She found a blacksmith to make her a sword of gold and prayed the legend was real. She waited for them to fall asleep and she sneaked into the house and surprised the witch and sliced off her head. The moment she was killed, the spell was broken, and her fiancé fell to the floor, realizing he had been bewitched to love her and the two ran through the town telling all who would listen that witches did exist, and what they needed to do to kill them. Suddenly, the fiancé started to feel funny, "What's happening to me?" she said and all of a sudden she flew into the air and screamed in delight. She had gotten the witches powers! When the town's witches heard, they gathered together and formed the Witches Council to protect all witches and to set rules to maintain their secrecy. The first ruling from the Council was that the new witch had to die for she knew how to kill them now, they also knew they had to burn the entire town to the ground and all humans in that town needed to be destroyed so that their existence would remain a secret. A spell was cast that barred anyone from leaving their cottages; they were unable to leave.

Their homes literally became their coffins. It was a swift death of raging fire with barely enough time for them to know what was happening. It was horrific, yet merciful in that they did it quickly, the only thing they could do to preserve their own. That night was the end of the town. The homes, the church and the schoolhouse turned to ash along with the towns-people asleep in their beds.

"We will meet in the fields and elect a Council" one of the witches said. They all gathered under the full moon and it was decided that the 12 eldest witches would set the rules and run the Council for eternity. That night the rules were set in stone:

1. *No Witch can show or tell a human about their powers*

2. *No Witch can bring a human back to life if they die*

3. *No Witch can cast a love spell*

4. *No Witch can go back in time and rewrite history*

5. *All Witches will be given a fair trial if a rule is broken*

6. *The Council will set the punishment to fit the crime*

Even though they have eyes everywhere, I know I can keep her safe and I'll never tell her what we are and I'll age myself as she gets older. Witches reach full grown at 21 and we only have to age if we want to. My parents only aged because they felt they should be a little older to have kids. Plus, the humans would notice if we didn't.

The next day as Mary and I were walking through the fields I stopped, grabbed both her hands in mine and said "Mary, do you know how

much I love you? I want to share my life with you."
There in the fields I got down on one knee. "Marry
me Mary. My parents want me to marry another
and have set an arranged marriage in place for me,
but I don't love her, I love you Mary." She cried
and admitted that she too was promised to
another. "Oh Declan" she cried, "I was afraid to tell
you, that I am promised to William, I was afraid
you would leave me." I shouted, "No Mary! I can't
let that happen I love you too much to lose you
now!" "I love you too Declan, but what can we do?
My parents and I had a long talk just last night and
they warned me that I have to marry William
because they need the dowry and they're
depending on that money." "We'll run away and
elope." "Tomorrow after church we'll have to stage
a fight and make it look real so that both our
parents will be happy thinking it's over between
us." "Declan, I don't know if I can do that." "You
have to if you want us to be together, do you want

to spend your life with me Mary?" "How could you doubt me, Declan? I love you so much my heart hurts" "Okay, so let's do this!" We pledged that we would: Our hearts and souls were one; now and forever.

After church we played our parts and had a huge fight, I yelled at her for being too bossy and she cried. "Declan Patrick Foley," she shouted, "I never want to see your face again." I should have won some kind of award for my acting abilities. "Good" I said "Because I want my life back without a bossy girl trying to tell me what to say and what to wear. If I'm not good enough for you how I am, then I'm glad it's over." Our parents were shocked for a second and then you could see the relief in all their faces. Only Joseph wasn't smiling because he knew the truth and he wasn't happy to have his sister leave town, but he understood or so I thought. We then decided to wait a week to get both our parents off guard and not to give a hint as

71

to what we had planned. It was the longest week of my life. I couldn't stand not seeing her, not kissing her not feeling her heart beat next to mine. Saturday May 6th came too slow. It seemed like the Council and the Gods were against us too, as it was raining that night, coming down like the wrath from the heavens. The rain was so thick, I swear I could've cut it with a knife while bolts of lightning were cast down all around like fiery swords, and I could hear the crackling of trees being hit in all directions. I climbed out my window and down the dirt road running towards Mary's house in town. She was sleeping when I climbed in her window and whispered "Mary my love, will you run away with me and marry me tonight?" She opened her eyes and jumped from the bed and whispered, "Yes my love I will marry you tonight. I've waited all day for you to come to me."

We climbed out her window, with Mary carrying a small bag holding a few belongings she had packed anticipating this night. We ran as fast we could. She tripped a few times on her long night dress getting caught up by her shoes, which kept slipping off due to no time to lace them properly. With only a light robe over her shoulders, the rain was really pelting down on her small frame as we raced away from our homes. The lightning was getting worse. I wish I could just magically pop us out of here but I can't. We were running as fast as we could without completely losing our breaths when suddenly, an extremely loud clap of thunder erupted and with that came the lightning bolt that would tear my world apart and start my journey. Mary fell to the ground and I knew she was hit and she was dying. I couldn't help her; the Council would know and kill her anyway.

"Think Declan, think," I shouted aloud. A spell that would keep her spirit alive not her body but her spirit, her soul, yes that could work. She was barely breathing, but she is still alive and that's not breaking the rules, she not dead not yet. I knelt down beside her holding her in my arms and I whispered softly in her ear, "I love you Mary Elizabeth Griffin don't leave me; don't ever leave me." She whispered back, "I love you more" and passed out from the pain. I gasped and felt the fire in my eyes as I started to chant:

> *"We love each other Soul to <u>Soul</u>,*
> *since the day my heart you <u>stole</u>,*
> *We will always find each <u>other</u>;*
> *death will not keep us from one <u>another</u>.*
> *Each time you draw your last <u>breath</u>,*
> *it will not mean your <u>death</u>,*
> *Twice the <u>heart</u>, even when we are <u>apart</u>,*
> *Your soul will be <u>reborn</u>, again and again;*
> *our love will never be <u>torn</u>.*
> *So with all my <u>power</u>,*
> *let this not be your final <u>hour</u>."*

I held her in my arms, and kissed her softly on the lips, as I started to cry, the tears poured down upon her cheeks. She struggled for air and I felt her body shudder as she faintly let out her last breath. I could feel the life drain from her body as her hand fell to the ground. "NO" I shouted to the sky, "damn you all!" I could only hope that the spell would work and that our love didn't die with her. I prayed I would find her again when she was reborn. I'll know her eyes, I thought. I'll create a locating spell to find her. I'll take her locket and use that to find her in the future. I didn't break any rules, I didn't save her life and technically, I didn't rewrite history, our history is still to come and we are destined to be together for all eternity. The Council can't interfere with this, can they? I left County Galway that night never wanting to return.

5

Maggie Benoit

I remember like it was yesterday, it was the winter of 1690; I was wondering around the states and found myself in Massachusetts after using the locket and creating a location spell to find Mary. Even though the calendar clearly showed it was indeed winter; the air was damp, cold but not frigid on this New England night. I'm thankful there's no snow on the ground yet; don't need that added chill running through me. A good stiff drink would warm me up or a pint of Guinness, I thought as I walked down Boston's Main Street searching for a welcoming sign, and there it was!

Sullivan's Pub: A typical Irish- American meeting place with its rustic décor, welcoming laughter and sounds of glasses clinking. Some people were standing by the large stone fireplace feeling the warmth of the crackling fire and chatting away telling stories of their youth while others sat by the bar looking tired and beaten down from life. Sure, I could have used magic to conjure up such a drink and bypassed this place all together, but I was trying not to; desperately trying. Magic was like a drug and I was an addict on the wagon. As I sat on the bar stool staring at the bottles of liquor lining several shelves; some so old I remembered the brands from long ago; I thought - what's next? I've never gotten over what had happened back home. I needed a break as I had been traveling for years and could feel myself becoming weary of life in general. If it hadn't been for the tingle in my bones, I would have just gone to the inn. I had to keep searching; it was the only thing I lived for. Then I heard it...the voice of an angel says, "What'll it be? Would you care for Beer or something stronger?" That voice made my blood hot and the hairs on the back of my neck stand at attention, that smile, I thought I was dreaming, but there she stood all 5'6, 110lbs, red hair and the greenest eyes that I'd only seen once before, they seemed to actually twinkle when she spoke. "Cat got your tongue?" she said. "I'll have a shot of whiskey, it's mighty cold out there; what's your name, Miss?" "My friends call me Maggie but you can call me Miss and don't be getting any ideas; I'm not for sale." "Let me start over I said quickly, I was just trying to be friendly. I wasn't trying to be crude. I couldn't help but stare at those twinkling green eyes. Can I buy you a pint to make up for my rude behavior? (I laughed)." "So you think you're funny now do you? Just because you have that fake Irish accent you think all the girls will melt at your feet." "Fake, it's not fake, Miss Maggie, I'll have you know I was born and raised in County Galway, Ireland." She threw back her head and let out a hearty laugh. "What century?" "Folks I know in Ireland don't talk like you, well, maybe my grandparents did 50 years ago." (If she only knew how right she was; I was from 50 years ago). "Miss, where's your manners? Here I am this lonely man in a new country and you have not a kind word for a brother?" I got up to leave and she yelled "WAIT, come back here, you're right. Forgive my manners, my mom and dad would kill me." I smiled and went back to the bar and finished my drink. I tried to make small talk the rest of the night but she wasn't interested. I had to find a way in. The shot had helped to take the chill out of my bones, and so did Maggie, just seeing those green eyes again, melted my heart the same way it did every time I saw them. I figured I shouldn't push my luck and I left and walked back to my dreary little inn room, which sat in back of a larger modest home. I shouldn't complain, as rooms were difficult to find if you didn't know someone, but apparently my appearance was trusting and pleasing and I was able to secure this place. A fairly comfortable bed with a colorful quilt and feather stuffed pillow was the only bright spot in this room. An ash filled fireplace kept it warm, though I had to keep stoking the fire to keep it going through the night. With one window overlooking a dead winter's garden area by day, my gaze drifted to the gray walls with flickering light from the fireplace each night to amuse me. One might even see witches dancing by the moonlight reflecting on it if you stare at the walls long enough! A large, over-stuffed chair with a thick wooden trunk holding my belongings completed the room. I could do worse; at least I have a roof over my head and hope in my heart. The spell worked and she was back. Things were beginning to look up.

This cat and mouse game went on for weeks. I would go to Sullivan's every night and Maggie and I would speak of Ireland and how homesick I was. She said that her ancestors came from Ireland, also. Little did she know how very right she was, but it was closer than she knew. I would get lost in those green eyes of hers and the scent of her hair as it whipped past me as she would jump up to tend to another customer, she smelled like a field of lavender in bloom just after a light rain.

Maggie was well respected by the townspeople, probably due to her engaging smile and innate kindness. When people would come into Sullivan's and speak of their spouse or mother being ill with chest congestion or some type of ailment, she would quickly make up a concoction of various teas, rum and wild honey with some bitters added, and tell them to drink it hot, a good amount of it, and then tuck themselves into bed with their covers up over their chests. Within a day or two, they would claim success with all symptoms gone! Whether their cold symptoms simply just wore out or Maggie did truly have the right "medicine" within the herbs of the tea or the warm rum and honey running down and soothing their hurting throats, who knows, but as long as it worked, people were happy, especially Maggie who hated to see anyone or anything suffer. Another reason I loved her so much.

After nearly a month of our bantering back and forth, she finally agreed to let me escort her out for dinner; a date. It was Saint Valentine's Day and the town was having their annual Valentine's dance. Even the foot of snow falling on the ground wasn't going to stop this dance. Back in the day, things didn't get cancelled because of snow. People just plowed through and enjoyed it. They were bundled up so that only their eyeballs were showing, and the children were always outside building snowmen or forts. As I walked down the street to her house I was getting excited to see her and to spend the entire evening in her presence. I will get to hold her and dance with her until the clock strikes 12. I am getting nervous and anxious at the same time about our date. It has to be perfect. As I knocked on the door, my palms were sweating and wondering what the hell I was doing, when she opened the door and there she stood in the most beautiful emerald green dress that caressed her figure like an elegant enchantress. I was stunned, I never believed she could be more beautiful than when I first laid eyes on her, but I was dead wrong. Be still my heart, it was beating so loudly in my chest I was afraid she would hear it. The green in her dress made her eyes look even more radiant than before, if that were even possible. Maggie had a way of looking at me, through me, inside me, and that thrilled me, yet humbled me at the same time. The evening was just as wonderful as I had pictured in my head all day. We danced and laughed all night long. Just holding her close to me was more intoxicating than any drink at Sullivan's – Maggie was my true elixir of life.

As the small quartet played sweet, melodic tunes, we danced, we talked and we laughed as I politely held her in my arms...forever the gentleman. Unfortunately, not everyone was as gallant, some jerk tried to cut in but I gave him a case of the hiccups (yes, magically). I fell off the wagon big time tonight. From then on every guy who tried to cut in I did a little magic jolt to them. I had fun, and I actually enjoyed using my powers, letting them loose, finally. Even though Maggie was the magic for my soul, but, just for laughs and to keep her to myself, I was not beyond sophomoric humor to give some guy a dash of clumsy feet, a case of stuttering so bad he couldn't get the words out to ask for a dance or an urge to hit the bathroom! I Declan Patrick Foley, was having fun for the first time in years! Yes, fun!

Later after the dance I walked her home. I offered her my arm, in my gentlemen's way, and she easily slipped hers through mine as we strolled down the street. How I loved feeling her close to me. I loved the way her hand fit in mine.

The lights in the homes we passed seemed to blink with approval at our passing by. As we approached her house, I dreaded that this night would soon end. We stood on her front porch for a bit talking and then she said "It's late, but I had a grand time." I wasn't sure if I should, but I leaned in for the goodnight kiss, lightly touching her hair, her face, and to my surprise she let me kiss her on the cheek goodnight. We both looked at each other a little flustered. I wanted to draw her to me, to press her body next to mine, but dared not – not yet. Oh, how I loved this woman, but to her, I was someone she recently met, with no memory of our past life together. I bid her goodnight and returned to my tiny room, but for the first time in more years than I care to remember, I didn't feel alone or sad. I had my Mary back again.

I finally had a purpose. Now I could settle in, get a job and become part of the community; wherever Maggie (my Mary) is …I will be there too. I heard there was work available through Henry O'Toole, a jovial, large man, who shared many local stories with me over an ale or two at Sullivan's. We felt a kindred bond between us, and thanks to his recommendation, I was able to get a job as the local blacksmith. Throughout my years I had learned many trades and studied with the best, and being a blacksmith was an honorable position in town, plus I liked working with my hands and melting and molding irons. It helped to calm my mind. I also loved being around the horses; they were better than most humans. I could be myself around them. I had one special horse, Red, her hair was auburn red like Maggie's and she greeted me every morning with a loud bray, and I swear a smile! I wonder who *she* was in a past life. I know that Red and the other horses sensed the magic in me but they didn't judge. When no one was watching I would pull an apple out from behind my back or give them an instant bath with a spell that left them shiny clean and odorless. Red really liked that because she hated pails of water dumped over her and being scrubbed down. That must be a clue, she was probably a cat in a past life, I thought and started to laugh. One morning as I came in I heard a noise and went to investigate and there was Henry with his back to me talking to Red. "Now girl don't worry this won't hurt a bit," with a wave of his hand and a few mumbled words she was shoed using magic. "HEY' I said no fair; I can do that too." Henry rose with a jolt and said "I don't know what you're talking about. I don't know what you think you saw but" he began to trail off "What do you mean you can do that too?" I let out a belly laugh, "I knew there was a reason I liked you." With a wave of my hand the blanket floated into the air and landed on Red's back. "Declan you're a witch, too?" "Yes, you don't have to worry. You didn't break any rules, the Council won't hunt you down and kill me." "That's not funny" Henry said as sweat poured down his face. "Don't joke about the Council. You know how it's been around here lately. With all the talk of witchcraft I suspect the Council will investigate soon." Henry said.

The townspeople or as I like to call them, the humans, never questioned magic before and now they think everyone is a witch. I've heard rumors that farther North they were stoning people they thought were witches. How ridiculous, any witch could not be stoned, they would just cast a spell and turn the stones to feathers or snow. They would never let themselves be captured, yes how utterly absurd. Thankfully, they didn't really know how to kill a witch.

Maggie and I have continued our courting for over a year now. All very proper with at least one or both parents sitting nearby while at her home or always a room filled with friends and strangers if at Sullivan's. As long as I could talk to her and sneak in holding her hand or an occasional kiss, that was fine with me, but now, it's time. I want her to marry me and tonight's the night I will ask her. I took her out to a fancy "eatery" for this incredibly special night. A beautiful Tavern called "The Cranberry Inn" was the place to go if one had enough money! It was a large brick structure with a fieldstone fireplace that stretched out over one entire wall. Impressive! It was one of the nicest buildings in the entire area, owned by the O'Reilly family who made their wealth in brick making and iron trade and then passed it on to their children who now invested in fine eateries and inns. The main dining area was called "The Lafayette

Tavern Room" and showcased sprawling, scenic murals on the walls painted by local artists. The oil lamps and candles on the tables cast a golden, magical hue over the place and even onto Maggie's already lovely face: She knew me well, "Declan, is something wrong? She asked. "No, I am just mesmerized by your beauty my darling" "I know you too well. What's wrong?" "Maggie, I wanted tonight to be special, we've been dating for a year now, well a bit over a year" "I don't always say the right things, I'm not good at that, but I do love you." She gasped as she saw him pull the little black, velvet box from his pocket. "Oh Declan," she exclaimed. As I got down on one knee, I said "I never thought I could love someone as much as I love you. I've loved you since that night in the bar. I can't imagine my life without you. I want to wake up every morning and see those sparkling emerald green eyes staring back at me. Margaret Ruth Benoit will you marry me?"

My heart stopped as she paused, then she started to cry, "Is it too soon, do you not feel the same as I?" I said. "No, it's not that, she finally spoke, I love you too Declan, I love you more than I can say and I wasn't sure if you really felt the same way that I did." Impatiently, I blurted out "Is that a yes?" "Yes, yes, yes, I'll marry you!!!" Tears of joy were streaming down her porcelain doll-like cheeks, and I couldn't believe my luck, my good fortune to finally have such love back in my life. My Mary, now my Maggie; how I loved her so. "I love you Maggie!" She replied, "I love you more."

We spent the next six months planning the wedding, her parents and brothers and sisters were making all the preparations. We decided to get married in a catholic church in Salem near where her parents lived, on June 1, 1693, Maggie always dreamed of being a June bride and having a huge wedding. The plans were set, she would wear her mother's wedding dress, her father had already picked out his formal tuxedo, her brothers were ushers, and her sisters were bridesmaids. My parents were coming from Ireland, my sister Orla as well. Unfortunately, Shannon & Maeve couldn't make it. I've warned them that there is to be NO MAGIC here in the states. Knowing that things seemed to be getting worse in Boston with the witch hunts, it might be best if we moved to Salem; I told Maggie that I wanted her to be closer to her family and she accepted that it made sense – thankfully! Her parents had always wanted her to stay close to home but she had ventured out on her own. It was unheard of at that time but they knew she would just run away if they did not agree. They finally agreed on Boston because of her Uncle John Sullivan who owned the bar and would keep an eye on her. I was able to secure a job with the local blacksmith in Salem and set up shop. I told Maggie to quit her job and just worry about the wedding plans and I would take care of the move.

I bought a small, stone house for us on Essex Street, where some of the homes were large and grand looking while others were neatly smaller but still regally placed. A good, safe street and neighbors seemed friendly enough. I told Maggie it was my wedding present to her and that she could decorate anyway she saw fit. And that she did! With hardly any money at all due to help from her family, they began fixing up the place with lace curtains, sturdy furniture and even flowering plants along the walkway. A happy project was in full force even before the wedding! They wanted us to come home into a place that truly felt like a home; and we were both so grateful for that.

It was May 6th now and spring was in the air: I can smell the faint scent of the early blooms of Wild Lupine and Meadow Roses blowing in the breeze. The wedding was less than a month away and I was getting anxious. I was FINALLY going to be happy. I was finally going to have happily ever after. I loved her and by some miracle, not magic, she loved me too. That should have been my first warning sign.

It was just a typical spring day, I was at work and heard lots of street commotion going on outside, but minded my own business as always. The townsfolk were in an uproar more so than usual. The regular pattern of the day was broken when Maggie's sister, Emily, came running into the shop screaming "Declan, Declan they've come and taken Maggie, they say she's a witch and will hang her at noon in the town square to make an example out of her." I jumped up holding a horseshoe and blazing hot iron in both hands, and looked to the church, the clock tower said it was 11:55. I dropped my tools to the ground and ran through the town desperate to save her and not knowing what I would do when I got there. I just kept thinking I have to get to her in time, I have to, it can't end like this. I can't lose her, not again, I won't, not this way. I raced past the people on the street their faces a blur. I don't care if they think I'm crazy. I know I must look like a madman, with terror on my face while kicking up the dust from the street and even knocking over carts, but I don't care, I only care about Maggie. I hear the whispers and I run faster and faster I must save her no matter what I have to do!

Even if I have to use magic, I will save her and God have mercy on those who try to stop me.

As I came around the corner to the town square, people are walking away shaking their heads: some crying in fear. "NO, NO, I shout, am I too late?" I pushed and shoved townsman out of the way. Then I turned to look at the tall oak tree, I could not believe my eyes. Through tear filled eyes, I could feel the rage building in my gut to my very soul, there she was, my porcelain doll, Maggie. Her lifeless body was dangling from the tree, she was wearing a pink dress and her red hair hung over the rope, her head was hanging down lifeless as one of the executioners were cutting her down. I rushed to her side but alas I was too late to save her, no spell would help her now, she was already dead. I fell to the ground; too angry to cry, though my eyes were burning and my body boiling with rage! I felt the fire growing in my eyes. Furious and outraged I turned to face her accusers and executioners. FOOLS! "You are all fools! "Now Declan, calm yourself, we had proof. Raymond saw her using magic she used potions to heal people; from the devil I tell you! We don't blame you; you didn't know what she was doing behind your back." Judge Regan claimed. "WHAT PROOF? You have proof?" I shouted, "Every last person that you have killed were not witches they were mere mortals like yourself. "

"You can't hang or burn a witch; they would laugh in your face and disappear in a cloud of smoke never to be seen in your lifetime again! I will not hide any longer this time you have gone too far. I will show you a true witch!" I bellowed at the top of my lungs. As the fire within me grew so did the fire in my eyes, as I spoke, one of the executioners, Raymond Bennett saw the flames in my eyes burning bright red; he died on the spot of a massive heart attack. His mouth still open in shock he dropped to the ground. I raised my hand as my eyes blazed with fire, angry and dead inside to even shed a tear, not caring about the Witch's Council as I yelled out in a bitter deep voice

"I call on the Powers that be,

destroy thine tree,

as I will so mote it be!"

As I chant this, the great oak from which Maggie died, starts to split down the center, the crackling noises grow louder and louder as it shattered like a thunderstorm brewing from the inside out, flashes of light spew from within and then with a loud banging thud as it fell to the ground. All of the onlookers gasp in disbelief and look terrified at me. Suddenly, the tree burst into flames. "I am a witch, I am what you fear, you should fear me and my kind, we have had enough innocent blood shed to last a lifetime. I tried to stay out of your mess but now it's personal and I won't be quiet any longer, you've gone too far this time, much too far," I hear my voice shrieking, "You made it my business. You see what I can do to a tree just imagine what I can do to you or your loved ones, the ones you hold dear. I can snap their neck with a wave of my hand. Just imagine what others like me can do in large numbers. We will never allow this to happen ever again. If one more witch trial is held or if one more person is killed, in anyway, I Declan Patrick Foley will destroy all of you and all your kin just as easy as that mighty oak tree."

Shattered and utterly destroyed by Maggie's

death, I walked over to her picking up her lifeless body, holding her close to me, as my tears begin to fall like an endless rain and spill onto her face, I whisper, "I love you Mary, I will wait for you until I find you again. You run through my blood, you are my life." All of the townspeople are screaming and rushing to their homes, they mumbled to themselves "I knew they existed, I knew it" over and over again, once safely inside they were never to speak of this again in public or private, never did the word witch cross their lips again. As I carried Maggie to be buried I placed her in the grave and said, "I'm so sorry Maggie, that again I couldn't protect you, but we'll be together in another lifetime." "I'll wait for you. I have no choice I can never love another." That same day, I left Salem forever.

6

<u>Dating Sarah</u>

I can't dwell on all the other Mary's; I have to concentrate on Sarah. So far everything that I've done isn't working. I've tried wooing her, sending her flowers; who knew this Mary would be allergic? Both Mary and Maggie loved roses. Boy was she mad when she saw those 12 beautiful long stemmed roses.

I've never seen a woman get angry over flowers. She used to love them. Back to the drawing board... I guess I'll need to find out more about her without seeming like I'm stalking her! Maybe I should talk to Joan and see what Sarah

100

likes and if that doesn't work; I'll just have to follow her around invisibly to see. An invisible stalker? Well, I'll do what I have to so we can be together ...again.

It's 10 a.m. and I'm running late as usual, Sarah thought, as she raced to get to the store. The construction crew was there today putting up the sheetrock and she wanted to thank her landlord, Mr. Hardy, for not only moving so quickly on everything so she could reopen in another month, but for also being brave enough to allow her back in that space due to the nature of the fire. The fire chief and police captain did determine that it was indeed arson, due to a Molotov cocktail being tossed into the store. A poor man's grenade they said. An investigation is still ongoing but the Benson boys were cleared, as they had a strong alibi of being at home that night; punished for some mischief they caused at their place, which both parents and a neighborhood friend could attest to. Though, Amy Santiago was considered a person of interest at this point. Mr. Hardy, a well-spoken, kind and hardworking construction builder, who dabbled in real estate, said he would not allow Sarah nor himself to be intimidated by cowardly bullies and felt what took place is behind them now and that the authorities would find and prosecute whoever did this. At the very least, no one would try to do this again now that the authorities were on high alert to anyone who looks or says anything suspicious about Sarah.

I don't know why I'm so excited to get the store back up and running; Sarah thought, people were afraid to come in, and now, with a fire and all...I can just imagine the rumors! Joan and I will need to think of ways to get back on our feet and to keep the doors open or I'll have to let Joan go completely and that's the last thing I want to do. Joan, with her wispy, light blond hair and golden brown eyes has been a very good friend to me since high school. I can't imagine owning this business without her being there; even though someday she'll leave to open her own bakery. When that day comes I'll be happy for her and all she's accomplished - through hard work, long hours and working both at the bakery and my store.

We met for tea at "Common Grounds" in the center of Branford, by the town's green, which is dotted with several historic churches with high, majestic steeples. Not just another small New England town but my home town. It's similar to Guilford along the Connecticut coastline, but just a few miles south. We ordered our usual Vanilla Chai Teas and one chocolate chip biscotti for me and a lemon one for Joan. They offered extensive coffee and tea varieties along with freshly baked desserts. The place was decorated with original artwork by the locals, and had a sprinkling of spots to sit. Wooden chairs, overstuffed comfy ones too, and even a couple of small sofas with coffee tables to place your orders on.

We always hoped to get the comfy chairs to sit and chat. Some days we did and at other times the place was so jammed with people sitting, chatting or deep into their iPads; we would sit at their small, round glass tables outside; weather permitting. Today, we lucked out! We sank into the soft, high backed chairs and placed our biscotti's on the table in front of us while we cradled our warm mugs in both hands sipping on the hot and delicious sweet teas: "Joanie, thanks for meeting me today, I know it's your only day off from the bakery but we have to think of something to bring the customers back in next month when we re-open, any ideas?"

"What about holding a séance?" "Seriously? The townies are freaking out already and that would really push them over the edge! I can just see the Benson boys making ghost sounds in the back." "Alright, then what would you say to a fundraiser? We could do something to donate money to the fire department that saved you and the store. You could get that hunky fireman Lt. Foley; wasn't that his name? He can pose for a calendar" Joanie sighed. "Not on your life then he'd think I was interested in him and I'd never get rid of him. He's becoming a really big pain in the ass." Sarah said with a groan. "Sarah, give him a break how could he know you'd be allergic to the flowers?" Joan smiled. "It's not just that, he looks at me funny" "Funny, how so?" Joan said. "Like he's in love with me, how crazy is that?" "He doesn't even know me." Sarah replied. With a chuckle Joanie added, "And that's a problem, why?" "It's just creepy. It's like that guy Billy in high school that used to follow you around asking to carry your books. Remember you didn't like it at all."

After a moment, Joan said, "Well, I think you

should give him a try, he's gorgeous. He's nothing like that dork, Billy. If you don't want him, I'll take him." "Joan Reynolds, you're married!" Sarah said laughingly. "I was kidding but really, have you really looked into those baby blues? WOW! That's all I can say and you're crazy." Joan added. Sarah just rolled her eyes at her. "I am not going to sleep with a guy just because he has what my mother used to call bedroom eyes." "So you *have* noticed!" Joan said batting her eyes. Sarah groaned, "Of course, you'd have to be blind not to have. They are really something aren't they? I usually look at the eyes first and then check out the butt." "Well, he does have a nice butt, too." Joan said. "Joanie, you're incorrigible! "Sarah laughed. "I think I'm going to do the Astrological Society Fair this year. It's every 3 months and I can possibly draw in some new customers. I can read the cards and you can sell some merchandise, it's on a Sunday and I know it's the only time you get to see your parents but I would appreciate it if you could help with this. This way we can do a booth at the same time." Sarah said to Joan. "That sounds good to me when is the next one?" "I'll contact my friend Alisa who works the fair and find out. She's an excellent reader and a good friend. We met while we were in Italy and ran into each other at one of the fairs. It's just a good thing I have a ton of merchandise that had just come in at my house. What a stroke of luck the delivery guy goofed and delivered to my house instead of the store."

Later that day Declan saw the poster in the window of the mostly empty store, which was now filled with saw horses, slabs of sheetrock and tons of sawdust on the floor, that read, "Meet us at the fair and have your cards read for $1 a minute. See our new merchandise and receive a discount coupon for our store re-opening soon. Sunday, August 16th at The Keeney Memorial Center, 200 Main Street, Wethersfield, CT. "Fair?"   "She'd have to talk to me there if I were a paying customer." Declan thought. With a smile on his face and a song in his heart, he walked home. For the first time in a long time his apartment didn't seem so dreary. Waiting for Mary, the beautiful soul of the only person you're meant to be with, can be extremely depressing; but now, now, I have a chance again to get her back into my life, our lives, so we can truly live again.

On Sunday the 16th Sarah was a nervous wreck. I can't believe I'm doing this! Hopefully it will pay off. I've stayed away for years thinking I wasn't good enough but it's time to give it a shot, she thought as she dressed. She stepped out of the shower and walked over to her closet, "Decisions, decisions, decisions" then her eyes lit up as she spotted it in the back of her closet a short sleeve blue shirt with stars and moons hung in the back. She hadn't worn that in quite a while as she thought of it as too special to wear everyday so she saved it for special readings. "I have the perfect sterling silver rune necklace and earrings to go with it. Slide into a nice pair of black jeans and some black pumps and I'm good to go."

She stopped to pick up Joan at her apartment building, which was only a mile from her own place. My trunk and backseat was already packed with boxes of crystals, rocks engraved with inspiring sayings and various books which had been salvaged from the fire; luckily, I had them in the back room which was untouched by the heat of the fire, but they did have a smoky odor for some time afterwards, but on nice days I would bring them out to my little back porch area to let them air out which seemed to do the trick, plus with some of what was delivered to my house we'll have more than enough to sell. Thank God my lucky cards were at home. I had taken them home to do a reading for myself to try to get a sense of that Declan guy. The cards say he's a knight in shining armor, so I guess I may have to give him a chance after all. Joanie had some beautiful, velvet pieces of navy blue cloth with silver stars and moons embroidered on them, which will look very cool on our table! She also brought an assortment of Tarot cards, which she had stored away at her place. Between the both of us, we pulled out as much as we could salvage from the store and divided up the scarce inventory; and now we're bringing it all with us and hoping for sales and future customers!

The Tarot card selection was ordered just prior to the fire and we are both are so glad they were untouched, as they were from a new company that offered an assortment of beautiful, artistic work on each set. So many to choose from and we painstakingly chose ones to fit our clientele at the shop. "Did you bring the cards?" Joanie yelled as she was coming down the stairs. "Yes, though, I almost forgot them as I placed them in my bedroom closet the other day after taking them all out and placing the decks on my bed to take another look at each one – they really are exquisite looking, aren't they?" Joan agreed and said she hoped we would sell them all, but, to save a deck or two for them to work with. "Not to worry I have my lucky deck with me, thankfully they were at home. I'll use those to read as they may help calm my nerves."

The drive took about 45 minutes and they got there early to set up. The Center was purchased in 1893 to be the town's secondary school. It was Connecticut's first High School. After taking on many changes, in 1983, the town turned it into the Museum and Cultural Center. The Keeney Center has three gallery spaces, an education classroom, rental space, Chamber of Commerce office, a hall for cultural concerts and events. It was as she remembered it with its beautiful hardwood floors on every level. We made our way to the second floor to set up. Alisa Moore met us with open arms; she was one of the originals who began this

"Psychic Fair" many years ago. She was quite mystical looking herself, with long, jet black hair that cascaded down her tall, lean frame. She had warm and very dark brown eyes that seemed to turn upwards, almost in cat-like appearance, when she greeted us with a huge smile while leading us to our table against the back wall. As Joan and I laid out the tablecloth, we gently arranged the navy blue velvet squares over it to highlight some of our items; we set up the cards on one end, the jewelry in the center and the books at the other end. We had quite a selection, even with so much of our stuff being destroyed: We found one box containing earrings, necklaces, pendulums and even beautiful gold plated candle snuffers. I left Joan to start setting up my own table in one of their other rooms where the readers were. I started to wonder, what if no one signs up to have me read for them? I'll look silly sitting here with my hands folded while all the others are doing readings. No,

I have to think positive. I will have customers, I will!

The morning went on and yes, I had many customers. Every 20 minutes the bell ringer would ring the bell to let the people know it was time to change or that their 20 minutes were up. At the sound another smiling face would sit-down.

Around noon I had a break and went to check on Joan. She was laughing and smiling at a customer and showing her our collections. As I waited for her to finish I took a chair behind the table. "How's business?" I asked. "Wonderful!" she replied. "We've sold out of the pendulums. I gave them your card and told them to stop by or that we would be here in November, and we hoped to see them again." "Next time we need more of them as well as the books on Tarot and Birthdays." "That's helpful to know." Sarah said. "I've had a steady flow of customers as well. This is my first break since we started at 10am. Maybe I will run downstairs to see what my schedule looks like for the rest of the day." Heading down the stairway to the first floor she went over to the women taking appointments for the readers. "Hi, I am Sarah Spencer. I was just checking to see if I have anyone scheduled for this afternoon." "Hello Sarah, I recognized you from your photo. Yes, you do have several more scheduled. Your next client will be at 12:40pm." The woman answered. "Great, that will give me a chance to grab something in the kitchen to eat. Thanks." I said. I forgot about the photo I gave to put up with the other readers I thought as I headed back up the stairs to the kitchen to see what's on the menu. Hot dogs, pizza and donuts, oh boy! "I'll have a hot dog and a tea, please." The few tables were taken so I stood over by the door and leaned on the radiator while I scoffed down the dog and then went back to my table in the other room to get ready for the next round. I guess the time will zoom by and it will be 4pm before I know it. Shoot! I wanted to go to one of the workshops they had. Next time I'll have to remember to tell them I won't be available for that hour. I really wanted to go to the past life or how to cast a spell workshop.

It was 12:30 and I started to get ready for the afternoon sessions. I took out a few new decks and put away my lucky deck to recharge later tonight. I want to cleanse the bad karma out of them. Then out of nowhere I got a strange tingling sensation through my entire body. What the hell was that? At 12:40 the bell rang and my next client walked in and I almost dropped all the cards on the floor. Oh wonderful it's him. I thought as Declan swaggered over to my table wearing tight fitted blue jeans, a black dragon t-shirt and black sneakers. His hair was tousled like he had driven a motorcycle or driven with the top down. OH MY! He really is gorgeous and I really am in trouble, I thought.

"Hi, I'm your next client" Declan said softly in a most seductive manner. "I saw your sign in the store window and thought it would be fun to have you read my cards. I brought along a few of the guys to have you read for them, too. I figured you could use the help." "Since you wouldn't take any of my calls, I thought this might be better." "Did you?" she said slowly. "Yes, come on Sarah you can't stay mad at me forever, can you?" "No, have a seat you're wasting your 20 minutes." "No, we have 40 minutes. I bought your next 2 sessions. I figured you could read my cards and read my palm but I'll skip the tea leaves. Your sign said you do them all." She thought to herself how the hell can I get through the next 40 minutes looking into those eyes.

"Did you have a spread in mind or is this your first time?" Sarah asked. "I'm new at this you pick." I lied. "Would you like to shuffle the cards?" "And cut my own throat? No thanks you

116

can do that too." With a smile she began to shuffle. "Let's do a three card Past, Present and Future and then we can decide where to go from there." She placed the three cards face down and began to turn them one at a time while taking in each card. After several moments she began, "Your Past card is the *3 of Swords* (3 swords piercing through a heart) which makes me think there was a loss in your past; a deep sorrow. I'll draw another under to see if we can see what that is about. The *5 of Cups* (a man standing in a black coat looking to the ground with 3 cups knocked over and 2 cups upright) you could have regrets about the loss and it feels to me that it troubled you very much, you were very sad. Next, your Present card is the *8 of Cups* (a pyramid of cups a man walking away) you seem to be searching for something or someone. You've let go of the past and you're moving on even though it's painful. Let's take another, *The Star*, (7 stars in the sky and a naked woman

117

pouring water into a pond with both hands) this is the card of hope and renewal so there's also a healing of old wounds happening now. I'm thinking that you are trying to repair a past relationship. Lastly, your Future card is another *Major Arcana* card *The Wheel of Fortune* (A sphinx on top the wheel, figures in the corners of the card represent the elements, earth, fire, air, and water, the letters R. O. T. A - written on the wheel) this is a good card to have in your future it symbolizes that you will have good luck, good fortune and change is happening. I almost think we should stop there but let's draw one more. Well, Mr. Foley it's *The Sun* (big bright sun with a baby on a horse and sunflowers) the card of light, so happiness and love are coming your way. Some people think this is the best card to get. Well what do you think?" "I think you're a little too good at this. Why not draw one more card to tell you something about me?" "Ok" "*The Magician*, (a magician holding a wand with a pentacle, a cup and a sword on a table in front of him and a garden of roses and lilies) well, seeing as you are not an actual wizard I would say that you have the potential for gathering your resources to meet your goals. On this card you have all four of the elements or suits of the Tarot: Cups, Pentacles, Swords and Wands." As the bell began to ring the first 20 minutes came to an end, then she said, "Palms next?" Nodding my head, I agreed.

As she took my hand and placed it in hers I started to feel the heat between us building and as she starred at it for quite some time; I began to worry. "Is everything ok?" I said. "Yes, but I have never seen such a long life line before; so much so, that I thought I had the wrong line." "Your love line branches out many times, just how many women have there been Mr. Foley?" "Not as many as you think. I'm a one-woman man." I responded. "Well your palm doesn't lie and it looks to me to be quite a few, do you always get the girl?" she asked. "Only when I feel it and she sends me the right vibes. When I feel the heat and I can see it in her eyes. The eyes are the windows to the soul you know"

As the bell rang to end our sessions she was still holding my hand. Well, this is a good sign. I whispered softly and seductively as I leaned towards her, "You don't have to let go if you don't want to. I can buy off the next customer and stay another 20 minutes or I can buy the rest of the day but my friends might not like that." With a thud she dropped my hand like it was on fire. "No that won't be necessary I believe we've covered everything." "I know you have a long day today but would you consider having dinner with me tonight? You did say my luck was about to change. I would love to just sit, talk and get to know you better." With a sigh she said yes. "YES! Great, I will pick you up at 7:00 at your house. I'll let you pick the place." "Fine, 7:00 is good I live around the block from the store on" I lifted a finger to stop her "I know where you live it was on the report." "Yes, I forgot, how about The Stone House Restaurant? I would love some scallops." "Great I love that place, see you at 7." YES, YES, YES it worked! Finally, she'll go out with me, now I have to win her over completely. I can't let this opportunity get away from me or from us we need this time alone.

At 6:00 I was ready and waiting to pick her up. I don't want to seem too eager although I would have been there at 5:00 if I could. It's 6:30, and I'm off! As I'm driving to pick her up I start playing conversations over in my head. I don't want to say the wrong thing and get her mad then she'll never go with me again. Let me play this one safe; I'll ask about her job and her friends and family. My palms were getting sweaty as I reached the front door. She heard the car and raced to the window and saw him coming up the walkway and her mouth fell open. He wore a black casual jacket, baby blue shirt with a matching tie, black slacks and black loafers. She didn't want him to notice her so she backed away from the window before he could see her. He heart began to race as she thought how beyond handsome he was, but, more than that, it was something else that she couldn't quite put her finger on yet.

Just as I was about to knock, she opened the door and my heart started to pound, Lord she was breathtaking. She wore a yellow flowing sundress with matching yellow sandals. Her hair was long cascading her shoulders with gold dangling star earrings falling just about her shoulders. "You look beautiful" I commented. "Thank you" she responded. "You clean up rather nicely yourself, Mr. Foley." I extended my arm and she surprisingly took it and I escorted her to the car. I opened the door and she slid in. Running around the car to hop in she started to giggle. "My, my, Mr. Foley what a gentleman you are." She said in a fake southern accent. "I try; my mother taught me very well how to treat a lady, but can you please call me Declan, Mr. Foley is my dad."

We made small talk as we drove to the restaurant. It was going very well. We pulled up to the Stone House and I ran around to open the door for her. "I reserved a table by the fire for us. I hope you like it?" "Yes, I've sat there before with my friends." "I like it here; the food is excellent." She commented. "I come here for the ambience and the fact that they donate to various Community Associations and Charities." "Yes, I heard that" she said. "Let's eat I'm starving after the long day at the fair." The waiter approached and we ordered. I had the jumbo shrimp cocktail with fresh horseradish and she ordered the Caesar salad with parmesan crisp to start. We talked and laughed in between bites. We talked about our parents, our childhoods and I told her mostly the truth. As the entrees were served she said, "We come to this nice restaurant for seafood and you ordered the steak...what a man!" "I was raised on meat and potatoes; you can't be Irish and not eat potatoes." "How are your scallops?" "Delicious and so is the risotto & asparagus, your steak?" "Medium well just the way I like it" I told her.

After dinner we decided to go for a drive down to the water for a late night stroll. The beach was empty so we took our shoes off and walked along the edge of water in the cool, damp sand. Hand in hand we walked and talked about the sky, the bright stars, and all the while I'm thinking, I can't believe I'm with her, and if I don't stop thinking that I swear I'll either cry with joy or grab her up in my arms and devour her with kisses! I went back to my truck and took a blanket from the back; laying it on the soft sand away from the water's edge. "Sit and talk to me Sarah. Tell me anything." "What do you want to know?" We covered family and childhoods over dinner. "Tell me something no one else knows about you, any secrets?" She started to get fidgety and I thought what did I say? "I'm sorry, did I say something wrong?" "No it's fine. I don't have any deep dark secrets just a few phobias. I don't usually talk about them as I'm afraid to scare men off. But with you I'll make an exception. Maybe you'll see how screwed up I really am and go away." "Fat chance of that" I said. "I actually got close to one guy in college and starting thinking this could be the one but when I told him about them he said I was too neurotic for him." "You can tell me anything Sarah and I won't scare off so easily. I'm glad he ran off, this way, I won't have to kill him." I told her jokingly but I wasn't joking I never thought she would have been with someone else before as none of the other Mary's had other boyfriends. "Well" she began "Don't say I didn't warn you. My biggest fear is lightening I've been terrified for as long as I can remember but don't know why. I don't wear turtlenecks because I get the sensation of being choked. I don't wear many necklaces unless they hang far enough from my neck. I don't swim in any water, oceans, lakes or pools, as it makes me a little nervous so I usually just go in up to my waist. And lastly, I don't think this is a phobia so much as a life choice, I don't want children. There, you have it - all of them, all of my fears laid out before you like a horrible portrait of who I really am. I can't believe I told you. Isn't this what you're not supposed to say on a first date? Rule #1, I believe! You can take me home now if you want." I felt tears welling up in my eyes as she spoke and as she spoke I saw Mary being struck by lightning, Maggie being hanged in Salem and Catherine dying during childbirth. I can't believe she feels it all. "No" I said softly. "No, I won't leave you. I'll stay as long as you will let me. Come on, let me take you home."

She was quiet on the ride back to her house. "Sarah, are you ok?" I asked. "You don't need to be embarrassed with me. I really do understand." "Declan, it's just that I don't know why I am the way that I am. I've got two therapists and even tried past life regression." I almost drove us off the road. "What, when, why? What did they say?" I blurted out. "Nothing helped it, didn't work, I wasn't able to regress. Once I could see a girl walking in the fields picking flowers and someone was coming but I came out of it. One Halloween when I was about 16 some friends and I went to Salem, MA for a tour. I froze at one point in the tour and had to go back to the bus for the rest of the day. I don't know what happened. I started to get claustrophobic. I'm a mess, Declan, you really don't want to be involved with me." "Stop saying things like that. Sarah, I really like you and I would love to go out again." "I had a wonderful time. You know Declan we are adults and it is the 21st century. You can come in and stay with me tonight if you want to." This time I had to stop the car. I slammed on the brakes she began to laugh out loud. "Declan Foley are you that old-fashioned or dare I say a virgin?" Now, I began to sweat profusely. "No of course not to both of your direct questions." Then it hit me...she's not a virgin this time! Now what? Who do I have to kill? This Mary is going to give me a heart attack, yes indeed!

As they got out of the car they strolled to the porch holding hands. When they reached the door he swept her up in his arms and carried her over the threshold. As she started to protest, he gently placed his lips over hers, pulling her in closer. Embracing her, kissing her sweet tasting lips, he began to feel so many old and new emotions. His thoughts ran rapid yet all he knew for certain was how much he loved this woman, God, how he loved this woman and he was going to make love to her, for the first time in this body. Life doesn't get any better than this, he thought. I've waited so long for her. Patience, Declan, take your time, this is her first time with you don't let all that passion out yet. You'll scare her to death. She won't understand why you love her so deeply - so all consuming.

She thought she was dreaming, here was the most handsome man she had ever laid eyes on and he wanted her, really wanted her. She could see it in his eyes, those damn blue eyes that she tried so hard to resist. She was so taken with him and it had happened so fast. She trusted him and had no clue why. She didn't realize just how much she really needed him to love her until she had held his hand during the reading. The emotions that had flooded her made her body hot with desire. She had never slept with a man before, why him, why had she chosen him? Why was he so damn sexy? Why did she invite him in? Why couldn't she say no to him? Why did his lips feel so soft, so tender and so inviting? He felt so warm so loving so tender, so giving. His kisses made her hot with passion, she felt the heat in her breasts, heat rose in her belly and she tingled down to her toes with desire.

She wanted more, had to have more of him. No one had ever made her feel so much with just a look, just a kiss. Their lips fit together perfectly. Her hand fit in his just right. Would making love to him feel the same? This was the first time her body ached to be loved to be touched so intimately. Is this what Joanie was talking about? She couldn't imagine it could get any better than this. She was wrong.

When they reached the bedroom she didn't know what to do, she felt so awkward, so shy. She was afraid that she wouldn't do it right. After all, she had no experience to draw from. Sure she watched a least a thousand love stories, read countless romance novels, but this was real life. Heart pounding sensations were running wildly through her blood. The heat between them was so intensely hot. She began to think ... just follow his lead, do what he does. This is insane she said to herself, Sarah, just get a grip just be yourself if he doesn't like you for you then you don't want him anyway.

He could see all the emotions running through her face as he watched her go from aroused to panicking back to aroused. He spoke softly to her "Sarah, it's ok if you've changed your mind. We don't have to do this now. I can wait." "NO" she said quickly. "No, Declan I want you to make love to me. Please don't go." "Darling Sarah, I'm not going anywhere." I whispered as I walked over to her. She started to undress and I stopped her "Let me." As I kissed her softly I started to undress her.

Her skin was so white she looked so fragile; her naked body was so beautiful I thought as her dress slid to the floor. I held her close and felt her shiver as I whispered in her ear. Don't worry love, I won't hurt you. Tell me if you want to stop. As she relaxed she began to loosen his tie, then she reached for his shirt and slowly unbuttoned it. Tossing it to the floor she marveled at his naked chest.

What a handsome, beautiful man she thought and wanted to just touch him. She began to move her hands up and down the bare chest feeling his heart racing the same as hers. She smiled enjoying watching him squirm for a change. As they lie naked on the bed getting to know each other's body, the sensations raced throughout them both until it was unbearable. He gently climbed on her kissing her softly and when they both were at the breaking point he slid into her. Her body arched to him as they both moaned in pleasure. They made love for hours until both bodies climaxed at the same time and both bodies were spent.

7

<u>Doubts</u>

Weeks had gone by and now it was October. This morning as I awoke and reached for her I found she was gone. Frantic, I began to search the room only to find her standing by the sliding glass door, gazing out on this clear, crisp autumn morning. The first rays of sun beginning to touch the top of her hand, the one holding the cup of steaming hot Colombian coffee with just a touch of hazelnut and vanilla, the way she likes it. She's the woman I want to be with until the end of time I thought, and those thoughts always made me feel so sad; losing her was becoming an obsession, I fear. Someone more attainable, smarter or perhaps with more money could surely lure her away – or worse...what if something happens to her, like the others? I hate these thoughts that seem to creep up at the oddest times. Even worse, what if she figures out my secret, who I really was or what I really am. Will these crazy ideas ever leave me? I'm not one to be so insecure, certainly not about Mary, but I know this Mary is very different from all the other past Mary's, this Mary could really destroy me when she leaves this time. Dear Lord, please don't ever let her leave, I thought.

Observing her and wondering what she was thinking made me think too much about how long will it last, when will she get too close to the truth, when will I have to pack up if this starts to endanger her life? I feel so undeserving of this woman who could clearly have anyone she wanted! She could have her pick of men, why me? That doesn't really worry me. I'll just get rid of anyone who tried to come between us with a spell.

But, am I being selfish? Could she have a better life with someone, anyone else? It gnawed at me, stuck in my mind, who was the first guy she was intimate with? I will find out and deal with him someday but not now, now I want to enjoy what we have for as long as it lasts this time.

Yes, Sarah Spencer was a catch alright, and right now she's my catch, my soul partner, so pull it together Declan, I thought. As I lie there pretending to be asleep, she walked quietly back to the bed with her bare feet and lavender silk robe clinging to her body. Not wanting to disturb him, she placed her coffee mug gently on the nightstand. He's magnificent she thought, as she watched him sleeping. From the right side he looked regal, his tanned skin was golden, his dark hair even after sleeping all night, fell perfectly into place, his arms were strong and lean and his tall body engulfed the length of the bed while his feet stretched over the bottom of the bed frame. Their lovemaking was better than any movie and way better than any dream could have been, more than she could have ever imagined. His body was the perfect fit to hers. They synced. He was hers and she knew she could keep him if she wanted just by the look in his eyes she could see how much he loved her. After making love with him every night since the very first night there was no doubt that they did belong together. He was hers and she was his. When did she start to feel so possessive of him? She had told herself she wouldn't let this happen. What if an old girlfriend came back or he just left and moved on to someone else? No, don't think like that she demanded of herself. I've never been this jealous in my life she thought as she sauntered over to the bed. "Declan, sweetie, it's time to get up, are you going to sleep all day?" "Sarah, sweetie, I'm up, he said laughing." "I couldn't help myself I was just watching you looking out of the window and thought, if she thinks I'm asleep maybe she'll come back to bed" "Not a chance, it's late", she giggled as I pulled her on top of me. "Didn't you get enough last night? "Never!" "I love you Sarah Spencer, and I'll never get enough of you." This time she laughed, "I love you more." as I rolled on top of her. As he began to kiss her she thought what the hell and they made love again in the morning light.

Each time was like their first time, always passionate and hungry for each other as if they both feared it would be the last time. After they both showered, Sarah dried off and went into the bedroom and stood by the mirror; she dropped the towel to the floor and began brushing her long, damp red hair. Stepping into the room in just a towel, Declan walked to her ever so casually as if he could sense what she was thinking at all times, and caressed her firm stomach, which felt so sensual and comforting to him as he gently began to touch her face. His touch was so electric to her and she almost fell over as he grabbed her into an embrace and began to kiss her neck and pulling her tighter to his chest. He softly touched his lips to hers as he stroked her breasts. "Dec", she laughingly called out, but he wasn't paying attention to the sunrise any longer, he was focused on her, her body, her smell, oh, how he loved that fragrance on her long, fair skinned neck. His eyes began to turn black with desire as he was holding her now in both arms, her brush fell to the floor as they began to melt into one another, his lips felt so hot to the touch it made her lips throb and swell as her body ached for him.

"Oh no, you don't! That's cheating!" Sarah cried out. "What is? All's fair in love and war." Declan murmured with his face burrowed into that savory neck he loved so much. "Dec, we have to go, you have to go!" "Do you want yet another suspension? We've already made love this morning and had sex in the shower. That's it for now. Save some of the passion for tonight." She desperately tried not to make eye contact with him because if she did, she knew they'd both call out sick today and stay in bed making love all day.

His eyes were a deep blue, sometimes like the proverbial ocean, but most times like a sparkling rare gem, and framed with his long, dark eyelashes, oh how she would've killed to have lashes like that, and those eyes would indeed make them late as they were intoxicating to her. As if his mind was just waking from a long dream he suddenly tossed his head back and said, "Oh, no, no, no! I forgot about the meeting today!" Sarah pulled him away and tugging on his arm. "Go on big boy, your captain awaits you! Hey, why don't you ask Tyler if he wants to go on a blind date with Joanie? I think the two of them may hit it off." "I'll show him a picture and let him decide and stop playing matchmaker." I yelled back to her as I walked out the door. Little did Sarah know that this meeting was about to change their lives forever.

On his way to the station Declan felt the sensation before he smelled the smoke or saw the flames. As he rounded the corner he saw that the top left corner of the Middle School was on fire. Flames shot out one room while smoke engulfed the entire building. Are children and teachers still in the building? I have to check. The trucks must be on their way I hear the school alarm now. I can't wait, children are in there! A boy came busting out the door running and screaming, his teacher I assume running behind him, "Connor, stay with the others! Don't run off without your fire buddy." "Hell with that!" he screamed back at her. Just as the others were pouring out all of the doors, I saw lines of children between 10-14 years old were in a line behind their teachers but others were running wild. As I try to get their attention I yell, "Don't panic folks, I am Lt. Foley from the Guilford Fire

Department. More firemen are on their way. Do you know how many are still in the building? Is anyone in any of the rooms on the top floor? What rooms are up there?

Just then I heard the scream, as I looked up to see a little boy at one of the top floor window. Tears streaming down his face, he cried out, "I'm trapped, somebody help me!" I have to get to him I can't wait. Here we go again, I thought but it's for the right reasons. I start to chant

"Into the smoke, don't let me choke;

to help the others I must protect,

I command the smoke to deflect."

As I race to the top floor kids are still running by me, "Get outside now!" I yell as I race by them. The smoke is getting thinner as I climb the stairs. As the winds pick up and blow the smoke away from the building. The room on the top floor with the boy trapped is in flames sending embers floating toward the ground as I hear the other arrive, firemen worked to contain the blaze to one side of the building. Just as I bust down the door I see the ceiling begin to collapse, I shouted to the boy, "Son, come here I'm a fireman, come to me and I will get you out." "I can't, I'm too scared to move." "Now! Before the floor gives way; the ceiling is about to fall." I can't wait. With a wave of my hand the boy is passed out and in my arms. As I jump the stairs racing to get him out I can hear the fire dispatcher with the department confirming the structure was collapsing internally as they moved closer to work on controlling and containing the blaze from outside.

A TV crew had gathered outside and I could hear the reporter say, "While initial reports suggested high winds may have played a factor in the dissipation of the smoke and flames, they experienced wind speeds of no more than 10 mph, and that heavy winds were not expected. There is no actual reason as to why the smoke cleared out of the school so quickly. I take you now to the school's gym teacher Mr. Arnold, Mr. Arnold, can you tell us anything?" "I was coaching basketball in the gym and then, just this noise, sounded like fireworks. Like sporadic noises. I told the boys that we needed to leave the building as the fire alarm began to sound. We just ran, went to the door and saw the smoke and just ran outside. The evacuation went smoothly, although there was smoke in the stairwell and the sound of the alarm scared the children."

Later at the station Chief Ryan bellowed, "Foley get in here now. Shut the door." Like the guys won't be able to hear him screaming at me. "The reason I called you in today was to discuss your behavior. Judging by today's fiasco I was right. You ran into that school without calling it in or waiting for backup to arrive. You know better than that Foley. This isn't the first time either.

What about the fire where you saved the little girl? AGAIN, you went in without Vega; he's your partner for God sake. How do you think he'd have felt if you died? He would have blamed himself. What if the baby died? You'd have blamed yourself. What about me and the men who ran in to save your ass? I'm done, Foley, you need some serious help with your Superman hero tactics. Hell, even Batman had Robin, all crime fighters - have partners and firemen are no exception to the rule." "I'm not seeing a witch doctor." I smirked. "I have no choice but to use you to set an example for the other men. I will not tolerate my rules being broken. I'm not your damn father, I'm your Chief and you will abide by my rules! You are officially suspended without pay until further notice. Get out of here and don't come back until you see the staff psychologist, Dr. Drake." "No way Chief, she's a woman." "No Dr. Drake, then no job." As I walked out the Chief followed me to the kitchen.

"Listen up men, Lt. Foley is under suspension until further notice. If anyone else gets any crazy ideas, you will join him." Tyler yelled as I was walking out, "Dec, better brush up on your cooking skills while you're out."

How am I going to tell Sarah I got suspended? It's not like I need the money. I'll have to say that I inherited the money so she doesn't get suspicious. Maybe it's time for us to get away somewhere maybe a cruise.

8

<u>Joseph Riley Griffin</u>

Sitting here I can't help but think of growing up in Ireland. It was great. I loved the green fields and the animals on our farm. I loved my family, too. Ma and Da were the best parents a child could want. I am also a twin. My sister Mary was taken from us too soon from someone I thought of as a friend. I feel like it was only yesterday instead of centuries ago. I began to think back to that night that our happy home was destroyed. As, I lay in my bed I'm remembering hearing the thunder and lightning pounding and crashing; the very ground shook from it. We had small rooms with very little furniture to help cushion the sounds from outside, but nothing would help the thunderous sounds from this storm, not even if we lived in a castle! I could hear the rain cascading down the outside walls and wondered if Mary was okay.

As I walked into her room I noticed that her bed was empty and she was nowhere in sight. She's gone. I knew she was going to run off with Declan, I just knew it! I would need to find them before they did something crazy or before Ma and Da woke up. As I grabbed my coat and slipped into my boots, I jumped out my bedroom window. Running through the meadow I noticed the thunder and lightning was getting worse like the Gods were having a ruckus. I couldn't see a thing and had no idea which way they went. But, knowing Declan, I took a guess that he would be heading towards the next village; he would not be aimlessly running off, he would have some kind of plan in mind. I was certain that I wasn't too far behind them too, so I kept running. After what seemed to be the biggest bolt of lightning I ever saw, I heard something. I was hoping no one was hurt; please, let my sister be okay, was my only thought. As I ran towards the sound, I could see Declan on the ground beside a body and to my horror it was my sister Mary. She lay there very still, she's not moving and I can't move either.

Suddenly, I felt a tightening in my chest, a gripping pain that intensifies with each breath, and I could feel myself falling to the ground as if in slow motion, and becoming detached from my body. I can't breathe; I'm not breathing...then darkness.

1688: Boston, MA I can't believe I turn 16 today! I woke up this morning feeling a little funny not myself today. At first I didn't even recognize my own room, it felt like I was waking up from a dream, where the dream was more real than where I am now. I quickly go to the basin and throw water in my face, wash up, get dressed and head off to school, but all I'm really thinking about is the party my parents are throwing me tonight at 6pm. As I walk to school like I have for many years now, passing by the same homes, the same roads, yet, something is not right. I feel like I'm in a strange place like I don't belong here...but somehow I'm knowing where to go and what to do. That's just crazy! What the hell is going on with me today? "Hey Raymond, Happy Birthday!" I hear as I walk into the classroom. Raymond? That's not my name, is it? I feel very confused like my name doesn't fit anymore. "Raymond over here," Tony yells. "What's wrong with you?" "I don't know I'm feeling off today." I replied. "Tony, I don't know what it is but I woke up this morning not recognizing my room and the way to school today. Just now when you yelled to me, I thought you were talking to someone else." "That's odd; maybe people in your family go insane at 16." Tony laughed.

This went on all day until I thought I would go mad. Am I bewitched? Christ Jesus, what the hell is wrong with me? On my way home from school I saw a mother playing with her twins in the park. Hmm something familiar about that I think and as I start to walk away I hear her say. "Joseph Riley, come here you're too far away from me." I turn with a jolt is she calling me? Confused I continued home. I race up the stairs and lay on my bed. I need a nap, what a day I'm having. As I sleep I dream of a land far away, very green and of a little red haired girl.

1690: Dear Lord, I'm 18 today and can't believe it. Let's hope it's nothing like my 16th. "Happy Birthday, Raymond" "My son is 18; it's so difficult to think of you as 18 years old already – you are a man!" my mother says as I come down to breakfast. "Your father has a surprise for you. He said to meet him in town before you start school. We're so proud of you, son." Heading into town I see my father outside the town blacksmith's barn. "Over here Raymond. I want you to meet someone." My father shouted. "This is the new blacksmith, Declan Foley." As I take his hand to offer a friendly shake, with that contact at that very moment our hands touch, memories flooded into my head into my heart into my soul.

Declan, my childhood friend, no that can't be, where's Mary I think to myself. "Raymond, what's wrong son?" "Nothing, Da, sorry I was daydreaming. What are we doing here?" "Your mother and I bought you a horse for your birthday." "Thank you this is such a surprise." I say as I am bursting at the seams. I have to get out of here. I don't know where all these memories are coming from like it was me but it wasn't me. I looked totally different in my thoughts. Hold on, this is like two years ago when my name sounded wrong and the mother in the park, with the twins.

Mary! She's my twin. I watched her die. Declan killed her. This Declan he looks exactly the same not a day older. I have to calm down, get a grip on myself, and ask some questions without looking like madman. "Pardon my manners; Mr. Foley is it? Did you and your wife move to town recently?" "No I'm not married." He replied. So Mary did die that day and he has no idea that I'm really Joseph. "I'll be on my way, thank you again." Pull it together Raymond, no it's not Raymond it's Joseph, Joseph Riley Griffin. My God what happened to me? Was I bewitched in some way? I must have been reincarnated. I've read about this kind of thing but if that's true then how can I remember my past life?

The next few months I spent researching. I spent all my free time going to the library combing through book after book. I found that people are starting to believe there are witches among us. That has to be it! Declan must be a witch! I have to expose him to avenge Mary's death. Maybe then I can find peace and go back to being myself again. Maybe if I kill him it will break the curse he put on my family. How? Where do I begin? I heard that he's engaged to a school friend of mine Maggie Benoit. I'll start by talking to her to see if she knows anything, maybe if I look different, maybe Mary does too, and just maybe she's really Mary. I sound like a crazy person, even to myself, but I don't have any other explanation for all of this.

Maggie was hanging clothes in the yard as I approached. "Morning to you Ms. Benoit" walking up to her. "Why are you so formal, Raymond? We've known each other for years." "Now that you are betrothed I thought it proper of me to use your surname." "Gossip has it that you'll be marrying Mr. Foley soon." "Yes, we couldn't be happier." "There's been talk around town that he may be a witch of some sort. What do you think of these accusations?" Horrified she turned to me and began to shout, "Raymond Bennett you be quiet! Don't say such things that could get him killed. Where did you hear such nonsense? I would know if that were true and I can assure you, Sir, it is not." "I'm just repeating what I've overheard around town." I don't think she knows anything; she looks really startled by the accusation. I know Mary and if she were Mary she'd be trying to turn it around on me and saying I must be the witch. No she can't know what's going on. As much as this will bring me pain I have to tell the city council that she is in fact a witch and I witnessed it with my own eyes and see what happens next. I wonder...will I die again? Or, will Declan tell the truth about his treachery. Whatever happens, so be it.

Christ Jesus! I never expected them to hang her. Now what will I do? Now it's me who has hurt my family. Here comes Declan; this isn't going to end well. "FOOLS! You're all fools!" Declan was madder than I have ever seen him. I hear Judge Regan say, "Now Declan, just calm yourself down, we had proof. Raymond saw her using magic. We don't blame you son; we know that you didn't know what she was doing while you were away at work each day." With those words Declan turned to me with his eyes blazing red, no they were flames of fire. I felt the pain in my chest strangling me. Oh no, not again I think. Is he killing me or am I dying again because Mary did. Those were my last thoughts as Raymond Bennett

1766: it's 10 years to the Centennial but today is my 16th Birthday. "Edward McGrath, get down here your breakfast is getting cold" "Coming Ma!" It's a fine day outside. The sun is shining the birds are chirping. Why am I feeling so strange? I keep feeling like I've done this before, but I didn't. I guess it's what they call déjà vous? It feels like I was someone else who experienced this a long time ago or in another lifetime. As I'm walking down the street I fall to my knees.

What the bloody hell is going on. Then, it hits me and everything is clear again. I'm Joseph Riley Griffith and I was re-born Raymond Bennett and now, yet again, I am re-born Edward McGrath this time. What the devil has Declan done to us? "If it all started in Ireland then that's where I'll go. He can't be the only witch out there. I have to find a way to break this vicious cycle. Damn you, Declan Patrick Foley, damn the lot of you!

I go along with this joke of a life with one purpose in mind, to save enough money to go to Ireland. After five long years of going without things and working my hands raw from cleaning out barns to hauling wood; I have enough and at 21 I'm old enough to travel. As I arrive in Ireland I feel a peace come over me. I'm home. Now what? How am I going to find a bloody witch and what will I do when I find one? I should look for a woman; she will be easier to get answers from. I can still charm the petticoats off them. Damn blubbering women will tell you their secrets if you smile and kiss them just right. Flowers won't hurt. How am I supposed to know who is and who isn't a witch? There has to be a way. I'll head for a pub and think on it. As I gulp down a few pints of ale I see something out of the corner of my eye. A glass moves across the table in the back of the pub and slides over to a beautiful raven haired woman. Can it really be this easy, have I found one that quick? How many pints did I have? The only way to find out is to go and have a chat with her. "Barkeep, give me a couple more pints" "Evening to you lass, I thought you could use another drink." I say as I sit. "Did I say I was looking for a companion?" she said with a sultry voice. "No, darling but I was." She laughed, "Have a seat; my name is Delilah O'Shea." "My name is Riley

McGrath." Why not, I thought, use my current surname and my real middle name which I always liked more than Joseph anyway. Yes, I thought from now on my name will be Riley. I like it! It has a nice sound to it.

That was the start of a very torrid affair. We would have great sex and discuss "what if" scenarios. The hotter the sex the more she talked. Good thing she's got a great body, great boobs and a nice ass and knows how to satisfy a man. Too bad she's a witch or I could really like her but she's a means to an end and nothing more. Night after night, she would tell me a little here and a little there.

"If there were such things as witches, mind you, that's not what I'm saying but IF there were they could never tell anyone, there were rules after all. Let's just say if there were they might have a Witch's Council to answer to. A coven that makes the rules some bad and some good for balance and if a rule was broken they would carry out such rules." It got to the point without her actually telling me they existed she told me everything I needed to know. She told me stories of how the only way you could kill a witch if they truly existed was to slice off their heads with a sword made of gold and if for a just reason the council might not come for you, they would decide your punishment if they really existed and she wasn't saying that they did. The more she was satisfied and the more she trusted me the more she said. She continued one night after a good 5 times I counted, "No Witch can cast a love spell or go back in time to change history so I've read somewhere. But I have read in some book somewhere that the biggest crime was to bring someone back to life after they die. Once their heart stops beating you can't bring them back." So I begin to play along with her and say "What if someone is dying and not dead and you find a way to save them, what then? Do you think the council would do something? If they existed that is." "I think it would be alright if they weren't dead yet, I think." "I also read that it if you were to kill a witch you would gather their powers, hypothetically that is." Realizing she has said too much she became very quiet. Absorb their powers, I thought, that's it that's the way to kill Declan. Finally, something I can use. I have to kill a witch in self-defense somehow and get their powers with a gold sword. Easy, nothing to it, I think. This is going to take time and some serious thought. If Mary dies young in this lifetime, I'll have to start all over again. I have to think of a plan before I die again and have to wait another 16 – 18 years to remember.

Joyfully, I am celebrating my 25th birthday today. I've learned as much as I can from Delilah these past 4 years. It's time to kill her and find another Witch. It's a shame. I have so enjoyed her mouth and body very much. She's taught me a great deal in the bedroom. She must have been a prostitute in another life, I thought with a laugh. The next time will be easier because I will be a witch and be able to know what I'm looking for this time. I have to get around the Council's rule. Start a fight with her in public and make her use her powers and I will just happen to have a gold sword in my hands and slice her head off. The Council will give me a pat on the back for saving their secret and let me in on everything witchy as I pretend to be shocked at my powers and abilities.

"Delilah, darling let's go to the pub to celebrate my birthday tonight. I have a big question to ask you one that will change our lives." I said. "Oh, Riley my love, I'll get ready and put on my most beautiful dress, just for you." I laughed as she left the room. Dumb witch thinks I'm going to ask her to marry me, I thought.

I'll be glad when this is over lately she's getting on my last nerve. It's all set just as she thinks I'm going to pop the question; I will tell her it's over. I'll tell her that her constant nagging has gotten the better of me and how bad she is in bed. I will really push her over the edge when I say that I've fallen in love with someone else and we are to be married. She'll never want to see me again, yes, that should do it!

That night as we walked arm in arm to the pub, we watched the other couples walking along the river. She looked happy and content. Entering the pub, it was crowded. Excellent! The more witnesses the better. I called for a few pints. Trying not to smile, I began, "Delilah my dear, I thought it only fitting that I bring you here to the place where we first met. We've been together for five long years. However, there's just no spark between us anymore." She began to look at me, tears forming in her eyes. "WHAT THE HELL DO YOU MEAN?" She screeched. "We have no spark? We have sex every day and every night. You damn well enjoy the things I do for and to you. How I degrade myself to pleasure you, how you make me feel like a prostitute but still I think maybe we're different than other couples but no spark, what the hell? I thought you brought me here to ask me to become your wife." "Wife, wives don't do what you do. I've found a nice girl in town and I've asked her to marry me. I told her I had to break it to you gently in a crowd. That I was a little afraid of what you could do to me."

"I'll turn you into a toad you damn little bastard, and I do mean little." "Toad, what are you saying, are you a WITCH! Were all those stories you spoke of real?" I acted shocked and outraged and a little scared. This is working better than planned. I noticed a man sitting in the corner watching everything. Could he be of the council she spoke of? If so, I better time this exactly right. "Get back, I say, show me your hands!" She began to rise as balls of fire formed in her palms.

People were screaming and running trying to escape all but the man in the black suit drinking his beer and looking ready to pounce on her. I thought I'd better do it now or lose my chance and have to start from the beginning. "Witch, if you are a witch and all the stories were true." I hesitate as I draw my golden sword and race to her. Just as she tries to hit me with a fire ball I raise my sword and swiftly slice off her head. Like Medusa or Marie Antoinette, her head rolls to the floor. By now everyone but the man has run from the pub. Jesus I think, now what, will he kill me? Just then I begin to feel strange, powerful, like a God. "Riley is it?" The man says. "I'll wager you're beginning to feel a little different. Just stay calm and we'll go to my room at the hotel and discuss what's just happened. No, no there's no sense in trying to escape. I will catch you. Let's talk before any bad decisions are made by either of us."

I walked with him, with a million things

running through my head. Stay calm, no one has a silver tongue like you do; I say to myself. You can talk your way out of anything. As we entered the dark and dingy hotel room he waved his hand and all the rights turned on. "Have a seat Riley. My name is John O'Rourke and I am an elder on the Witches Council. As you may have guessed by now, you are becoming a witch. You have killed a witch and her powers have transferred to you. What you say next will decide if I kill you or not. I can assure you that I have a great deal more power than you and I have used my powers for centuries, not minutes. Tell me what I didn't see." I was beginning to wonder if I had a chance so I began my story that I had spent many hours coming up with. "I met Delilah back in 1771, we became lovers. She used to tell me stories of witches, hypothetical stories. I never really believed her until tonight. Things were getting boring between us and I decided to break things off with her. You see, I've found someone else. Imagine my shock and horror when she said she'd turn me into a toad. I then realized in that instant that she was indeed a witch. I was fearful to say the least for my very life. I was trembling until I remembered a story that she once told me, the only way to kill a witch was with a gold sword. You had to slice off the head completely."

"And you just happened to have one at your side, interesting." "No, when I first heard the story I said what if the stories were true, maybe someday I'd need to protect myself. I am an expert at fencing. I studied a great many hours in my youth. The next day, I went to the local blacksmith and had it custom made. See for yourself, it has my name and the date engraved on the handle. I bought it a long time ago. I never expected to use it especially not on Delilah, a woman for God sake. May God have mercy on my soul." I added. "Well, Riley you do tell a tale now don't you? It all sounds very logical. Let me see the sword." As I handed it to him he took his time studying it. Then he began, "Yes, I can see this was etched a few years ago. So, I must assume that the rest of your story is true as well. The council has given me the power to make the decision and to exact punishment if necessary." As he stared at me with those evil eyes I sat on the bed terrified to see if it all was worth it and to see if I was going to get my revenge on Declan. "I will grant that this was indeed self-defense. Delilah should have kept her mouth shut about us and telling you our secrets. I will therefore, let you live. You know that secrecy is key to our existence and if you were to tell someone we will know as I will be watching you for a probationary period of roughly 100 years. I will give you all the rules only once so pay attention; you only know a few of them:

1. *No Witch can show or tell a human about their powers*

2. *No Witch can bring a human back to life if they die*

3. *No Witch can cast a love spell*

4. *No Witch can go back in time and rewrite history*

5. *All Witches will be given a fair trial if a rule is broken*

6. *The Council will set the punishment to fit the crime*

Remember Riley, the council will be watching and it won't always be me. We will send others from time to time." With a wave of his arms he was gone, vanished into thin air. I'd best keep my thoughts to myself. Smiling, I realized, I DID IT! I am now a witch with powers of my own. Time to start practicing, Declan, you'll never see me coming.

9

Ann Barrows

On July 9, 1835, two beautiful bundles of joy were born. Their names were Ann Mary and Andrew Joseph Barrows. The Twins were born into a wealthy home to the proud parents of Clyde and Bonnie Barrows (no relation). Dr. Barrows graduated from the University of Pennsylvania and practiced medicine in New Hampshire. His wife Bonnie was, as most women, a homemaker. Ann and Andrew were the only children to be born to the happy couple as Mrs. Barrows had miscarried the first three times. These twins were indeed a blessing. They were very close as the years went on. They loved to play together to the point of having no other friends.

Even when they started school they were inseparable. It wasn't until the teenage years that they started to drift apart. Andrew was not at all happy when Ann started to notice boys. He would threaten and scare them away. It had gotten so bad that Dr. Barrows had to have a man-to-man type talk with Andrew. "Son, why is it that you don't want your sister to have a beau?" "I don't know Dad it just makes me so angry, like I know they will hurt her." "I don't know where this comes from but it must stop at once. You are both about to turn 16. You need to start looking for a suitable wife for yourself to start a family after you finish school. Ann needs to think along those lines as well; she will need a man to provide for her as she has grown accustom to. I only want the best for the both of you as you know your mother and I are not as young as we used to be and need to know you are both secure in your futures in the event of our deaths." "Don't worry father, I will take care of

171

Ann if she doesn't find a suitable husband."

July 9, 1853, was a gorgeous day the sun was bright and the weather was warm. The twins were 18 years old today. Andrew was getting ready to go off to the University of PA to follow in his father's footsteps come September. His parents had noticed a change in him since he was 16. They couldn't put their finger on it but it seemed that he grew into a man almost overnight. His attitude about life had changed and he was hell bent on leaving town without Ann to attend college.

Ann had just graduated from High School with no prospects of finding a husband. She felt tired just thinking about her future and being introduced to potential suitors by her parents and their endless friends. She knew it was the proper thing to do and understood her parents concern for her future, but she just didn't feel a connection with anyone. There was no shortage of young, suitable men. Ann was aware they found her very attractive, with her long brownish red hair, 5′ 7″ and weighed 110 lbs. and she knew all the proper things to say, her manners were impeccable, but she had no desire to spend the rest of her life with one of them. Oh, the idea of that made her shudder! So, for today, she decided to take a break from even thinking about it and headed off to the beach with her best friend Victoria Billingsley. Victoria was the envy of all the girls with her long blond hair and sparkling blue eyes, they had met in High School and became fast friends. They seemed to like the same things; especially shopping. They both had a keen sense for fashion and loved looking at the new styles coming out and planning their outfits. Victoria at 5′10″ had long, lean legs that Ann envied as every dress seemed to fit her like it was made for her. While Ann was a bit shorter and is seemed that everything needed to be hemmed so she wouldn't trip on the fabrics. Victoria had just announced her engagement to the handsome Nathaniel Peabody. Ann was to be Victoria's Maid of Honor next February 14th. How she wished to find her true love. too. She often dreamed of a man with the deepest of blue eyes and the blackest of hair. She saw him vividly and thought that it was odd to dream of a man she had never met. He just made her weak in the knees to picture him. Every man that came to court didn't measure up to this man of her vivid dreams so she decided if she had not met him by her 20th birthday she would think about marrying Nathaniel's brother, James. After all, he had asked her, many times, as she frequently spent time with him when they double dated with Victoria and Nate. He was more of a dear friend to her, but, she also didn't want to become nor labeled a spinster. Andrew had been acting odd now for a few years, it must be a teenager thing. Just last week he didn't hear me call his name even though I had begun to shout. Then he said the strangest thing, that for a moment he wasn't sure that it was his name. Andrew not know his own name? How very odd! Then he asked me if I felt like that, too. Of course, I said no. Now he wants to go away to college, I'll miss him so very much; we've never been separated before.

As Victoria and I reached the beach we spread our towels out on the sand. It truly was a glorious day. We had all of the newest fashion and bridal magazines that her father had brought home from his travels to New York in hopes to nudge Ann in the same direction. This was going to be the talk of the town, a gala event to end all galas. I came upon the girls sitting on a blanket on the beach. My pocket started to vibrate I could feel the locket pulsate. Ah I thought one of them is Mary. I've found her again. Which one? I bet it's the brunette, I can't explain why but I feel a pull towards her. Now, how do I get her attention? I've got it. "Victoria what do you think of this one?" I said.

When all of a sudden a man fell onto my blanket, the sand was going everywhere. My hair and bathing suit were covered in sand. "You imbecile, can't you watch where you're going!" "OH dear, I'm so sorry I said with a sincere apologetic voice. Just run into the water and it will wash off." "Please, forgive me I tripped trying to catch the ball. My name is Declan Foley it's a pleasure to meet you." I said as I extended my hand. She began to wipe the sand from her face to look up at me when she gasped. OH my word it's him! The man I've been dreaming of for months! "No, no it's quite alright. It's just that you startled me, I'm Ann Barrows, Mr. Foley." "Declan, please call me Declan." Victoria began to clear her throat. "Mr. Foley this is my friend Victoria Billingsley. We were looking at Bridal magazines before we were interrupted. Victoria is getting married." "Please accept my apologies to you both for my clumsiness. This may sound crazy Miss Barrows but would you consider having dinner with me tonight so that I may apologize properly. I could come to your home and speak with your father before we go." "Well I don't know; we don't even know each other. For all I know you could be a murderer, sir. However, I assume you would not want to speak to my father if you were, she said with a shy smile. So, yes Mr. Foley, I would indeed love to have dinner with you. You can pick me up at 7:00 p.m., I live at 135 Clinton Avenue." "I'll be there at 6:30." Victoria looked at me with her mouth wide open in shock. "Ann Barrows, what are you thinking? You don't even know him. I've never seen you do that before. I've seen you turn men down hundreds of times but never give in that easy." "Victoria I can't explain it but you know about the man I've been dreaming about, well that was him." "What? No, it can't be! That only happens in books." And so it began from that first day, we became more than friends

Ann was excited and ran to Victoria's house. Screaming as she ran up the stairs to Victoria's room, "Vickie, Vickie I have news!" "What the heck is going on?" Victoria's father poked his head out of the bathroom. "Sorry to bother you Mr. Billingsly, I was looking for Vickie." "She's out in the backyard." "Thanks, and sorry again for yelling." Running back down the stairs and past Mrs. Billingsly she smiled and ran through the kitchen and swung the door open. Vickie heard her before she saw her. "What's going on? Are you on fire?" she yelled to Ann. "Vickie, Declan's asked my father if he could come over tonight to talk to him privately. TALK TO HIM! I think he's going to ask for his blessing to marry me!" Ann said, as she was jumping up and down. Victoria grabbed her and the two were jumping up and down together. In the kitchen, Mrs. Billingsley said to her husband, "Clyde, any idea what that was about?" "No, he said but they are teenage girls after all it could be a new hairstyle with them." Chuckling to herself she kissed her husband's cheek and said. "You see dear; you do understand women after all."

Later that night, I showed up at the Barrows home. This never gets easier I thought to myself. Asking to marry a man's daughter is really tough. How do I explain how much I love her to him? He doesn't know that we've been together in 2 other lives. I can't say, Dr. Barrows, you see Sir, Ann is really Mary, my true love reincarnated. I've found her once before in another time where she was Maggie. Don't let it bother you that Mary was struck by lightning or that Maggie was hung as a witch. Now, she's Ann and we are truly meant to be together. I dare not even broach that subject! Just trying to calm my nerves with a little humor to myself. As I gathered up the courage, I knocked on the door. Ann barreled down the stairs, "I'll get it; I'll get it." "I'll get it, it's my house." Her father said as he opened the door. "Come in Declan, have a seat. I hear you would like to talk to me privately. Ann, go on and help your mother in the kitchen with supper." "Yes dad" she said smiling to Declan as she raced to her mother. "Yes, sir." he said as they walked to the living room. As they sat on the sofa, I began to sweat. "Sir, your daughter and I have been dating for a while now and I think it's time to take the next step. I'd like to ask your daughter to marry me with your blessing, sir." Dr. Barrows looked at me with a furrowed brow and was sure taking his time to answer I thought. "What does Ann think about this?" "We've talked about getting married someday, but I would never ask her before talking to you first. I have a good job working on the railroad. I was also fortunate enough to inherit property in New Hampshire, left by a Great Aunt who recently passed on. It's a cottage in the woods with about two acres of land. This is the reason I wish to settle down." "Property you say? Well then Mr. Foley you have my permission to marry Ann, if she is willing to do so. I'm very happy you won't be taking her away from her family." "Ann, come in here and join us. I'll leave the two of you alone for a little privacy. I'll check on dinner." With a strong handshake and a smile, he left the room as Ann came running in. "Annie, my love, have seat. I've just inherited property in another town close by. I make a good living but most of all I love you and would like to start a life with you, if you'll have me. Ann Barrows, the love of my lifetime, will you marry me?" With that said, I pulled the small black box from my pocket and on bended knee opened it. The ring was white gold with a large one carat diamond. She squealed in delight and stuck out her hand. "Does that mean yes?' "YES, yes I'll marry you, Declan. I'm so happy." As I placed the ring on her finger I kissed her softly on the lips, as I pulled away I whispered in her ear, "I love you

Annie." "I love you more." she whispered back as tears of joy rolled down her cheeks.

The following year on May 6, 1854, we were married. I figured that May 6 had to be the day, it was the day Mary died and it was to be mine and Maggie's wedding day. I had to finally erase the bad memories and make that day special again for her and for me. Things would be different this time, this life.

And, this time when May 6th arrived it was indeed a glorious day. The sky was bright blue, the birds were singing and the flowers were beginning to bloom. I made sure of it with a little spell at midnight:

"Bright and sunny let this day be,

I beg you Mother Nature to hear my plea,

Of calming winds and flowing air,

Of yearning fire that magic flares,

Protect this day with all your might,

From early day to late of night!"

When the sun rose on that day, it was just perfect. Our first real life together, it had to be outstanding. This was going to be the first time Mary and I got to have a wedding, a honeymoon and the first time we would make love.

At the stroke of noon, we were married. I finally married my true love. There was no greater feeling in the world. I think we can make it this time. This life will be ours. Even though I am a warlock, I have to pretend to be a mortal so I couldn't take her somewhere exotic with a snap of my fingers. We decided to save our money and go to our new home. I had magically refurbished the log cabin house that was already there. Or course, I lied when I said I had inherited it. I couldn't say that I bought it when my instincts said she was here in New Hampshire. I kept it rustic on the outside as not to draw attention and enhanced the inside the best that I could so that life could be a little easier for Annie. The parlor had a huge couch with the softest of pillows. A piano in the corner as I know Annie enjoys playing. A desk and chair in the opposite corner for her to write her children's stories. I dreamed of evenings by the fire enjoying a good book while Annie played the piano. The bedroom was designed for a man but I had told her she could change it to her liking. I didn't mind, whatever made her happy. I had told her that along with the house came a substantial amount of money. I did it all for her even before I met her this time.

That night I carried her over the threshold and carried her through the house and up the stairs to the bedroom. As I lay her down on the bed I can't believe how lovely she is. This will be a first for us both. Nervously, I began to undress her as she lay there looking into my eyes. "Are you scared my love?" "No, I think I've waited for this night since the day we met." We began to kiss while removing all of our clothing, and I lied on top of her watching her eyes. As the pupils in her eyes began to dilate, the soft moans of pleasure came from her as I caressed her body and slid inside of her. She was so soft, so warm and so moist. I never knew such pleasure could exist. The passion and the fire at the same time rocked us to the core. We came at the same time moaning and groaning each other's names. I laid there a little longer not wanting to move not wanting to stop, just holding her and looking at her lovely face and those eyes I knew so well. As I rolled over we laid side by side kissing. "Oh Declan, my love that was wonderful; we are truly one now. I can't believe we're married and starting our lives now as husband and wife. You'll see, I'll be a good wife. We'll have a happy home with plenty of children. We'll spend nights by the fireside making love and planning." "Annie, I have everything I've ever dreamed of already. I can't wait to start building a family with you."

Alas that day never came. As the years went

on I was content that it was just the two of us but Annie became more and more saddened as time passed. There were four miscarriages and I thought I would die every time I saw the heartbreak in her eyes. Finally, in June of 1880 after 26 years of marriage Annie was pregnant. We had to wait until September to see if she could hold the pregnancy and even though she was now 45 the doctor said if she rested she would be able to carry the baby to term. September came and she was still pregnant at last we were going to have a child together. This Thanksgiving we would be very thankful for all the blessings we have in our lives. I worked on building the nursery in my spare time with a little magic here and there. Annie was usually resting, she rarely climbed the stairs to see what I was doing in the attic. These days she only climbed as far as our bedroom on the 2nd floor or we curled up together downstairs by the fire. I used the excuse that I wanted to surprise her and that seemed to do the trick. I couldn't let her see how fast it was coming together, as no mere human could do what I had created in such a short time. I told her I had hand carved the crib; added a long closet with doors for all the baby's clothes and made a rocking chair for her to sing the baby to sleep. When the baby comes I can carve his or her name in it between the two hearts on the front of the rocker. It was such a pleasure to use my magic for something so special.

Things started to fall apart in October when the snow began to endlessly fall. It seemed to be every day the damn white flakes wouldn't stop. The freezing temperatures didn't help it was so bad we had to stop the trains and shut down until spring as the snow had made the tracks impassable. The only saving grace was that I could be snowbound at home with Annie during the pregnancy to keep an eye on her and to keep her safe. It was getting so bad that the snow was reaching the second floor bedroom window. The first floor windows were completely blocked. I had to use a shovel and some magic to create a tunnel to the barn to check on and feed the horses. Luckily, she was now housebound and so was everyone else in town. No one would see or know that we were in better shape than others. By November, five months into the pregnancy, we were completely at the mercy of Mother Nature. Thanksgiving this year would just be the two of us by candlelight. I don't know how the others are handling this; if it weren't for the magic we would have starved or frozen to death. I thought of casting a spell on the whole town to save everyone from further suffering, but since the cold and snow was so widespread, it would surely draw attention if our town was the only one thawing. I did manage to fix it so that Annie's father found a frozen turkey in his yard. Not working gave me ample time to help where I could. I started the tunnel to my neighbor's house and he and I dug to the next until we were able to at least travel house to house. I had an ulterior motive; one of my neighbors was Annie's doctor. I had to keep him alive. What a year this has been! Electricity is discovered and used in home now only to not have any during this damn winter. Christmas was suddenly upon us but my only concern was keeping Annie and our child safe from the dreadful weather. I carried Annie to the nursery to show her my masterpiece. With tears of joys she said, "Declan, this is breathtaking! I can't believe you did all this by yourself. It's absolutely perfect. The baby will love it, too." "I'm so happy you like it but why are you crying my love?" I asked. She whispered "Because I don't have anything for you." "Me? You've given me the world. I have you and I have our baby. I don't need or want anything else. I love you Annie Foley." "I love you more." Was her response.

In January I noticed that Annie's face was red and she was very irritable; very uncomfortable. I ran through the tunnel to the doctor's house. "Dr. Lewis come quick Annie's not well." After examining her he said, "Declan, I have bad news Annie's developed high blood pressure. Her pressure is 200/110 and I think she may need to have a Cesarean to remove the baby so that Annie's pressure will come down. I can't give her medication as we've been snowbound for months and I don't have any to give her and it could harm the baby. My biggest fear is that she'll have a stroke." "STROKE, what the hell is that?" "It's the narrowing of the arteries of the brain that block the flow of blood to the brain." "Can you deliver the baby here?" "No, it's dangerous; we'd have to try to get her to a hospital the babies lungs aren't developed enough. If I deliver here we could lose them both." "OH NO! Not again, not this time. I won't let that happen." "Declan calm down, and what do you mean this time?" Just then Annie began to speak, "I've heard what Dr. Lewis has said. He has explained it all to me and I will not be delivering this baby now. I have to give the baby a chance to live. If our baby dies I won't be able to handle it. Declan, we've lived, our baby hasn't. I know you'll be a good father." "Stop Annie, don't say that." As we argued I could see the change in her face, her arm fell to her side sending the glass of milk to the floor. Dr. Lewis shoved me aside and said, "She's having a stroke. I'm sorry there's really nothing we can do because of the weather. It's just not possible to get her there. We'll have to make her as comfortable as possible. I can take the baby without permission. Seeing you are her husband, you can overrule her decision and I will take the baby and try to save her." What do I do? Do I cast a spell? I'm afraid to cast a spell on her not knowing if it would hurt her or the baby. I have to try something I have to save Annie I can't lose her again, even though Dr. Lewis said this is our last chance to have a baby.

Annie's body or mind can't handle it. If I do a spell and kill the baby? Annie may die of a broken heart and if I do nothing she will die from a clot or hemorrhage to the brain. "Dr. Lewis, take the baby now and save Annie." As the words came from my mouth, I watched her eyes roll into the back of her head as she lay helpless on the bed, dead again. "Declan, I'm sorry they're both gone. It was just too late to save them." Dr. Lewis patted me on the back as I fell to my knees aside the bed sobbing. As the door closed behind him I felt the anger rage though my blood. "Annie I'm so sorry I could not save you. I've lost you again. What do I do now? I'm so lost.

Out of anger, rage and sorrow, I dug a grave, even though the ground underneath the snow was frozen, I chose to use no magic, just my bare hands breaking away at the unforgiving cold that helped to steal my family from me. I dug until my hands were bloodied and blistered and every digging device was broken.

I wrapped them together, mother with child, using blankets and beautiful crocheted shawls and bedspreads her parents had given to us and carried her lifeless body outside through the private path I had made and buried her. When the snow finally cleared in March I conjured a Weeping Willow over her grave and I closed the house down. I left the nursery as it was. I left what could have been. I've kept it to this day and occasionally put roses and baby's breath on their grave. I don't know how many more times I can do this until I finally break.

10

<u>Catherine Duffy</u>

When I found Mary in 1921, she was strolling through the large courtyard of The Bellevue-Stratford Hotel in downtown Philadelphia. The courtyard was filled with women with large saucer-like hats with cascading flowers, and gentlemen with gold pocket watches dangling from their waist coats. Mary; I knew it was her the minute I saw her. The hairs on my neck were twitching, the locket was vibrating and there she was. She was wearing a long white summer dress, holding a pale green parasol to block the sun from her pale skin while her large white, plain hat highlighted her exquisite features. Her shiny black hair was upswept and elongated her already tall, slender figure causing her to look imaginary; it was as if she just stepped out of a rare painting. I walked over to her and said "Good Afternoon, my name is Declan Patrick Foley, if I may be so bold, may I ask what your name is beautiful lady? She smiled and her green eyes sparkled as she said "It's Kate, Miss Catherine Elizabeth Duffy to be exact." And so it began, again.

Thankfully, she always falls in love with me. I think it's because I love her so much and she always feels the love and sincerity that emotes from within my soul. My own eyes must give me away too. I can't help but look at her as though she is the only woman on earth and to me she is. I have never fallen for another because there is only Mary. No matter what she looks like, no matter what, I will always love her and only her. I am a one-soul man!

I swept her off her feet in a whirlwind

romance and we were married at Cathedral Basilica of Saints Peter and Paul on Feb. 14, 1922. She wore her mother's wedding dress which bore a 12-foot train, with pearls that seemed to endlessly travel around the front and back of her dress then up to the curve in her neck and down her arms. She was all lace and pearls. She carried a bouquet of soft, velvety red roses to mark the day, and later I discovered she also wore a red garter. She chose Saint Valentine's Day; a little cheeky, but I could never deny her anything her heart desired.

The church was filled with all of her family and their friends. While most weddings would be dwarfed by this Cathedral's majestic structure and vaulted ceilings, Kate's array of guests seem to overtake this architecturally eminent structure. The prestigious assembly included prominent bankers, attorneys, along with Kate's dear friends since she was a child, including her Nanny, Mrs. Templeton, who had eyes that seemed to smile at us. Kate's mother, Mrs. Duffy, cried during the entire ceremony and I swear Mr. Duffy was reluctant to give her hand to me but with all eyes on him especially hers he put her hand in mine. The priest spoke but I couldn't hear anything, my heart was beating so very loudly and I was waiting for the words to come, and I now pronounce you man and wife, you may kiss the bride. We exchanged white gold wedding bands and then it was time to kiss her. Back in those days you barely kissed a woman before you married her but I knew what I was missing; after all, we've had so many lives together already.

We were married for 2 ½ years when I came home for dinner one night to find her crying over burnt chicken. The kitchen had a layer of haze hanging in the air, and the small oven had blackened streaks on the white, porcelain door. I ran to her side and said "Kate, what's wrong my love?" "I burned dinner, she cried and this was supposed to be a special day for us. I can't do anything right and I'm getting fat." "WHAT! Never, I said. As I wiped away her tears" "I'd love you no matter what, burnt food and all, no matter how much you weigh, you are the most intelligent and beautiful woman I have ever met." "Well, I'm glad you feel that way because I'm going to get very fat, then she smiled and said, "Declan, I'm pregnant!" I felt my heart stop and fell to my knees by her side and cried tears of joy. I would have the honor of having another child with her. I could only pray for a longer life than the life that Ann and I had. "I love you Mrs. Foley." "I love you more, Mr. Foley." She replied.

The pregnancy was normal, we enjoyed every moment of it. We ate, we laughed and we were in awe of the baby growing inside her. We laughed out loud every time we lie in bed at night and felt the baby kicking. We decided on Declan for a boy and Mary for a girl. She picked the boy's name and I, of course, picked the girl's name: I told her it was one of my favorite Aunt's name that had passed away. I had thought of doing a spell to see what the baby was because in those days you just waited and were surprised, but I was afraid something would or could go wrong, and I would never forgive myself, so I decided to just be surprised. I wasn't surprised, I was devastated.

It was a cold winter's night on November 30, 1925, when she awoke in pain. She said, "I think my water just broke and I can't feel the baby moving, this is it." I felt the panic set in. I jumped out of the bed and threw my clothes on; they had been put out on a chair just for this purpose. I helped her up and grabbed her suitcase and rushed her to the car. I wanted so bad to just zap us there but I knew it would freak her out, she didn't know I was a warlock after all. It was snowing outside, everything was covered in white, and it was a dangerously, beautiful night as I gingerly guided her down the stairs. A fall would not be good at this time!

The drive was only 15 minutes but seemed like hours as Kate moaned in pain and I so wanted to relieve her from that. I left the car running as I carried her into the hospital. This was supposed to be the greatest day of our lives, the day we had been waiting for, our baby was going to come into this world and we would be ecstatic with joy, but alas, that was not meant to be. I never thought they would need a protection spell. It had been years since I've used magic and there was no sign of any problems. Dr. Lye walked out of the room and I waited for him to say it's a girl or it's a boy, but I was not prepared for what came next. "I'm so sorry Mr. Foley I did everything I could but we lost them both. The baby had the umbilical cord wrapped around her throat but when we tried to do an emergency C-Section it was too late; she suffocated before we could get to her. That's when Mrs. Foley's pressure started to drop and she started to hemorrhage, she lost too much blood and her heart stopped beating. I'm so sorry we couldn't revive her, she died on the table." I was numb and could barely hear the words he was saying.

How could a perfectly healthy woman die while giving birth? Catherine Duffy-Foley died Nov. 30, 1925 during childbirth.

I went into a deep depression wandering the countryside. My life felt over, but yet, I could not die. It was now 1938, and I found myself living in Connecticut.

I never told a living soul about my secret to this day, that I had been the cause of the devastating hurricane in CT that year. I had held in my powers for so long, wanting each Mary to have a normal life with me, and for what? I just didn't care any longer – my rage against life was overtaking me in a dark way.

I began experimenting on controlling the elements ...why not? I was waiting for Mary to be reborn again. I thought I could move the pressure in the air down far enough to cause a storm out in the Atlantic Ocean to increase in size, thereby, pulling the water up into this vortex and creating a storm, which is perhaps what I needed to get the anger and grief out of my soul. I wanted the earth to rage with me and then perhaps it would purge out of my being and I would be ready for the next Mary, and she would be ready to be reborn. I didn't know if I could do it, as the elements are very difficult to maneuver even for the greatest warlocks who roamed this earth for thousands of years. I've moved small portions of lakes before and caused some local, minor flooding, making certain never to harm anyone, not even the land. This was supposed to be an experiment far enough from land yet one I could feel and see in the distance that was small and contained, so not even a boat would be harmed. But something was happening that made me lose control. There was way too much wind and rain and emotions pouring out of me! It was crazy; the more I tried to stop it the more the sea rose. As the fire started to ignite in my eyes, I chanted an ancient spell to conjure the sea and the wind to join as one:

> *Let the sea take my pain,*
> *Let me feel the wind and rain,*
> *Let the water twirl, Let the waves hurl.*

I imagined it all in my mind first, a storm building over the open waters, the dark clouds swirling, the high seas spiraling and then I would have commanded the storm to rise! At first nothing at all happened, not even a bolt of lightning but then, something went wrong, it went very wrong.

As I started to walk home I heard something,

as I turned I could see way off into the ocean huge waves starting to form. At first I was impressed by the sheer force of nature I had created, but then the waves grew larger, like steel gray walls of water crashing into the docks, higher and higher. "OH NO!" What did I say, how can I reverse it? Quick Declan, think:

> *Let me take my pain,*
> *Stop the wind and rain,*
> *Let the waves hide,*
> *Let the waters subside.*

That was stupid, it's making it worse. The water was coming up to the streets. Think Declan, no more spells until you think this through. Get the word out like Paul Revere and warn people of the huge tidal waves coming.

But something inside of him was turning and churning just like the wind and the waves; he found a strange sensation within, one that he never felt before, not to this level anyway. He liked this dark, destructive power. It felt like the gates of hell were within him and that they were bursting open and pouring out his rage; his despair. He could no longer contain the ages of agony of missing his Mary, his soul mate. Declan wanted to rip the skies open and to let the sea reach up and swallow him, swallow the whole damn earth! He lifted his arms in the air while the rain drenched every inch of his body and screamed up to the heavens to take him, kill him, and kill everyone! "What's the use of living this soulless life? Why, oh, why?" he moaned and then fell on his knees in water rising all around him and the wind blowing so hard against his body he felt that it would levitate him off the ground. He lost track of time and place, as his body writhed with an aching so deep, he felt he would surely die this time, swept away, disappear, and he would happily accept his fate to end his agony. Come and get me, please, do it now he shouted to the wind.

In the distance he heard voices and then began to see light; people were searching for people, those caught up in the storm, his storm. He stumbled to his feet and was surprised to see the sky lightening, daylight, had he passed out there all night?

Men were scrambling all around lifting tree limbs off of people, names were being yelled out to see if they were alive. Out on the river banks which now looked like the Atlantic Ocean itself, people were on top of floating homes begging for someone to save them. Children were crying – children! Declan quickly got up and accessed the area; it was horrific. There were bodies floating; people walking around dazed, confused and sobbing for their loved ones, their neighbors. What have I done? What have I done?

Over the next few weeks Declan worked in makeshift emergency shelters to try to alleviate his guilt and remorse. Nothing worked. He tirelessly and with a new conviction in his soul helped each person he came in contact with. He walked the southern New England shore for months as the bodies continued to mount to well over 500 dead, 1,700 badly injured.

That was no storm, that was a full-fledged hurricane! To this date, in history, this was one of the top 10 ever to hit the United States. Declan declared to never forget nor forgive himself for causing this.

Magic is powerful and apparently my powers have grown over time. I must not let my feelings get out of control like that again and vow to help mankind, not to destroy it. I have to only use magic for good. It's the only way I can even look in the mirror.

11

<u>Loving Sarah</u>

After all the past lives of Mary, I've finally found so much happiness with Sarah. I can't explain it but I feel the connection to Sarah so much more than all the others. There's a knowing within me that I won't lose her this time, or perhaps it's my fears not allowing me to think otherwise. But, this may truly be her last reincarnation with me on earth. Scares the crap out of me to feel so much for her the only way to describe it is that she makes me forget all the rest like she's the first and only. I've been feeling this way for a while now and can't explain it. But God help me I love this woman to my very core. I've decided that when she dies someday so will I. I just can't do this anymore; I can't keep starting over again and again, not this time, I will make damn sure the council kills me or someone else. I'm beginning to think we'll never have children or maybe that's what triggers something in the spell. Maybe adding another life somehow activates the spell. I just don't know but both Ann and Catherine died before giving birth. Can that just be a coincidence? I'll have to make sure it doesn't happen this time, I can't let Sarah get pregnant it could be her death warrant. Then maybe just maybe we can have a longer life. Who would have thought my spell for all the right reasons would end up tormenting me and hurting Mary for eternity? Now to figure out a way to tell her I'm suspended indefinitely. Thankfully the shop closes at 6 and that will give me time to come up with something.

At 6 p.m. Sarah turned off the last light in her shop and stepped out to find Declan standing there with his hands in his pockets looking like the poor cat that just killed the canary. "Hi Sweetie, what's wrong? How did your meeting with the Chief go? I thought I would have heard from you earlier." "Love, do you want the good news or the bad news first?" "Bad" she replied. "Well they kind of go together. On my way to the station there was a fire." "Fire, are you ok? Tell me that's not the bad news!" "No, no I actually helped a school that was on fire. But I didn't wait for backup and the chief chewed my ass out. The bad news is I'm on an extended leave of absence." She began to give him that look. "So, the good news is that we'll have more time to spend together. Maybe I could build some shelves in the store for you or we could take a trip." Tapping her foot on the ground she said, "How do you expect to pay for a trip? I assume that means no pay either. Well, I do need work

210

done in the store and that may keep you busy." She said with a smile. "Don't worry about money, I told you that I have an inheritance from my Grandparents. There's plenty. Plus, I want to talk to you over dinner about something that's been on my mind." "OH?" "Not now, Sarah, over dinner. Let's go." As they strolled arm and arm down the street I began to sigh, "I love you so much Sarah it hurts. We'll get through this together." "I love you more and that's why we will." She said with a laugh. I've always loved the way she said that she loved me more, it gave me a warm feeling right into my very soul; a feeling that all is well and they have truly created their own Utopia on earth. If she only knew all that I've done so that we could be together. How I wish I could tell her everything. It feels like I'm lying to her all the time about who we really were; if she only knew all the lifetimes we've had together. How I've walked the earth for centuries to always have her in my life due to what

I really am. I could really do so much for her, for us, if I could just be myself and use the magic I was born with. But I was all too aware of the consequences of doing so, and I wouldn't dare risk losing her because of my own desire to share everything with her.

Sarah was busy fixing dinner in the kitchen while I began to pace the living room wondering how to approach the subject. She knew this morning that it would be a late night and defrosted the homemade sauce that she had frozen on Sunday. She decided on spaghetti and meatballs. It was his favorite besides corned beef and potatoes. She set the table with her best china. She giggled to herself, aren't you fancy tonight Sarah Spencer? Do you think it's what you've been wishing for? Do not get your hopes up Sarah, she thought, especially now that he's been suspended. A girl can wish can't she? I'm not going to be let down if it's not tonight. I have patience, I can wait.

I love him so much. I melt every time he looks at me with those beautiful blue eyes as if he's looking into my soul.

"Dinner's ready!" I moved to the kitchen and grabbed the dishes on the counter and walked over to the table. "What's the occasion for the elegant china settings tonight? I said, and leaned over the bowl to kiss her softly on the lips. "Well" she said "If you keep kissing me like that I may have to use them every day or we may just skip dinner altogether." I placed the bowls of spaghetti and meatballs on the table and pulled the chair out for her. "My lady, won't you have a seat?" "Don't mind if I do kind Sir." She laughed. As we enjoyed our meal and as she rose to clear the plates I stood to stop her. "No, no you cooked, therefore, I clean." I said as I bowed before her. Clearing the table and adding the plates to the sink, I said, "Have a seat and let's talk." "Ok, why so mysterious?" she smiled. "Well now, smiling at me like that is going to make me forget what I want to talk about." "I was thinking that the holidays are coming rather quickly and I was thinking of a Christmas wedding." She interrupted, "Christmas? You want to talk about Chris..." she trailed off as it hit her. "Wedding?" she stuttered. "Yes, but only if you'll marry me Sarah my love, marry me and love me for the rest of our lives. But wait, before you say yes, I have only one condition." As I knelt down on one knee and opened the little black box containing the biggest emerald she'd ever seen. "The Emerald is to match your eyes, although it could never be as bright." Before she opened her mouth to say yes she sat back staring at the ring, "Condition, what condition?" "Sarah, I've thought this though for days now and I know one of your phobias is having children, but Sarah, I don't want children either. Please, say that you can live without them, that you haven't changed your mind, please I beg of you. I'll never ask for another thing or ask you to go without again." As I waited with baited breath I watched the tears start to pour down her face. "Declan are you absolutely sure you can live without them? I haven't changed my mind and I was terrified that you were going to say that you wanted one." "No Sarah, I want what you want, everything that you want." "Then YES! I will marry you Declan and I have a condition of my own first, I want a New Year's Eve wedding. I want us to be married at the stroke of midnight and start the New Year off right." "Deal" I said as I slid the ring on her finger. "Declan, it's gorgeous but you really shouldn't have." "I didn't; it was my grandmother's ring. She left it for me with a note that said to give it to my soul mate. That's you Sarah, you're my soul mate. You're where my heart found a home. I love you Sarah Spencer." "I love you more." She whispered in my ear as we both began wiping the tears from our eyes. We fell onto the floor and made love and talked until the sun rose.

For the next few weeks I helped around the shop adding shelves to make room for the new shipments and fixing the old bookcase that was barely standing due to the heavy amount of books. "Sarah, you have to move some of these or I can't build you a new bookcase." "Declan, it's been standing there for two years now and with the reinforcement hinges you added it will last another two years. Sweetie, why don't you call Tyler and go for a beer or something? For the love of God go out and do something for yourself, please stop helping me. I love you for it but you're making me crazy." "Ok, Tyler's been calling to check in." "Then call him because I love you and still want to get married." "I love you too, so I'm going. Call me if you miss me too much." "I won't and I love you more."

I love it when she says that! It should be

weird that every Mary says that. I guess it's because it comes from her soul. As I pull the phone from my pocket and punched in the numbers Tyler picks it up on the first ring. "Dude, it's about time, I thought you died." "No, just getting under Sarah's skin so I thought you might want to grab a beer and fill me in on the station." "Cool, meet me at Casey's in an hour." As I hung up the phone I decided that it would be good to catch up. I pulled up to Casey's, a small pub that's always filled with neighborhood people or guys from the station. Casey's a short in stature big in heart type of guy with a full head of white hair and ruddy cheeks; he's always greeting people like they're walking into his home. He's got a nice little menu too with excellent food; you can't even find a seat in the place on St. Patrick's Day due to his corned beef and cabbage special…he's got a special touch with that! I got there a little early and figured I'd get a head start.

"Casey, a beer and keep them coming Tyler's on his way." "Declan, I haven't seen you in here for a while, are you whipped yet? Don't give me that look, I'm kidding, I'd be whipped too if I was dating the beautiful gypsy." Casey said with a smirk. "She's not a damn gypsy she's a Tarot reader." I said. "Yeah, yeah whatever, she's still damn cute." "Declan, when are you going to make an honest woman out of her?" Casey said as he poured the first round of beers. "New Year's Eve, we just set a date a few weeks back." I replied as Tyler walked in the door. "What's on New Year's Eve? Party? I'm up for it." "No, Sarah and I are getting married. That's why I asked you here to see if you wanted to be my best man." "Sure, after all I am the better man." Tyler smirked. "Great it's set then, a toast to you and to Sarah."

May you be poor in misfortunes and rich in Blessings May you know nothing but happiness from this day forward

Wherever you go and whatever you do,
May the luck of the Irish be there with you.

"What?" Tyler replied when I stared at him in amazement at coming up with such a perfect toast. "I looked it up – thought this day might come." Clinking glasses, I figured I better ask, "Is the Chief still pissed?"

"Yep, you really did it this time. He said you can't come back until you see Dr. Drake; the lady shrink. Go see her it can't be that bad. We miss your cooking. I haven't had a decent cheeseburger grinder since you left." Tyler said with a smile. "Speaking of food, how about a blind date with Sarah's friend, Joan Reynolds? Here's a photo of her." I said as I pulled out my phone to show him a photo of the girls. "She's cute, ok set it up." Tyler said with a wink. "Don't change the subject, what about Dr. Drake?" "Ok good I'll let Sarah know and we'll work something out. Dr. Drake, yes I've been thinking about it. Maybe I'll call and set something up. I have to get back to work or Sarah may cancel the wedding." I said with a laugh. We stayed for a couple of hours gossiping like two old ladies. I finally said, "Ok brother, I've had enough or you'll be carrying me home." "Get to the shrink and I'll see you back at work and we'll start thinking about a bachelor party." Tyler responded. As he walked out the door Tyler's smile turned to a frown. We'll just see about that Declan, yep, we will, thought as he closed the door behind him.

As soon as Tyler left I thought to myself it can't be that bad; I'll go talk to her put a spell on her and she'll send me back to work. Damn, why didn't I think of that before? "Hi, Dr. Drake, this is Declan Foley I believe you've been expecting my call." "Yes, Lt. Foley I have, my schedule just had a cancellation for tomorrow at 10am can you come in then?" "Sure Doc I'll see you at 10 a.m. sharp." Better go home and think of a spell quick. Nothing fancy, I've got it:

May you sleep the sleep of the deep,
Awake to find that I am fine
Never to remember the spell
That has made you think I am well
Back to work I must be sent
So that I may pay the rent.

I must be really drunk. Nevertheless, it will do the job. The next morning, I got up bright and early and headed to the doctor's office. It was a brick professionally building and her office was on the 1st floor. It must be so her clients can't jump I thought as I walked into her office. "Good, you're right on time, let's get started. Have a seat, do you prefer Lt. Foley?" "I prefer Declan." "Can I get you something, water or coffee?" "Sure Doc, water is fine." As she turned her back to pour the water into the glass I chanted the spell in my head and as my eyes began to change to flames she began to drop the pitcher. I was able to catch her before she hit the ground and placed her in her chair. When she awoke a bit frazzled she looked at me with sleepy eyes and said, "That was a really good session Declan. The Chief may have misjudged the situation. I am going to recommend that you return to work immediately." "Thanks Doc, I really think you've helped me. I'm sorry it took so long." I smiled to myself as I walked out the door.

12

<u>Revenge</u>

Tyler walked back to the station after having a few beers with Declan. Walking past the green he stopped to sit on the park bench. It's always so nice this time of night and I do my best thinking here. Going over in his head about the conversation tonight he thought "best man" is he kidding me? Now is the perfect time to finish the plan; I have to get this right down to the very last second, timing is the key to success. I have to succeed there's no room for error. If he even thinks something is off it will be over before it begins. I need the element of surprise on my side. Think, it has to go down at her place but

223

how do I get him to Sarah's apartment? Maybe I need to check her schedule see when they plan on having dinner or even better have them invite me over. I can make sure she has to go to the store for something she forgot. I have to make them think it's their idea to invite me. So it begins.

Tyler spent the next few weeks going over the plan in his head. It has to be perfect he repeated to himself. Get a grip, he said he thought nothing can be out of step it has to go like clockwork. With extreme difficulty he made sure not to act differently at work. He greeted Declan at the beginning of each shift as he usually did. Tyler made sure he laughed at his jokes. They worked in tandem on making breakfast; Declan scrambled the eggs and Tyler fried the bacon. Then they sat and ate together as they did every shift for the past year. Tyler would say the eggs were runny and Declan would say he burnt the bacon. They rode the truck together side by side acting like kids;

"Who's riding shotgun this time?" they'd laugh. They battled the blazes in brotherhood; always watching each other's back. Tyler began, "So Declan, we have to start making plans for the bachelor party. I was wondering how far you want me to go with it. How about a sexy girl that pops out of a cake or stag movies? I hear there are some really great ones." Declan almost choked, "You hear? I think you mean you own a stash of them! I know what an animal you are. I've heard the stories about your women; how they can't resist your charms. No, let's just get the guys together and go to the bar. We can have a few beers and shots and shoot some pool. Or are you afraid of losing to me again?" Declan replied. Tyler smiled, "Sounds good to me. I just hope the guys can get away to come seeing it's the holidays. Nevertheless, on December 30th, we will have a great party. I can't believe you're getting married on New Year's Eve at the stroke of midnight. Nice way to ring in the New Year. And by the way, I let you win at pool since you outrank me. That won't be happening this time." Tyler continued, "We could always go to Vegas." Tyler said with a smile. "How is Sarah doing, any pre-wedding jitters? Are the plans coming along ok?" "If you're so concerned then why don't you come to dinner next week and see for yourself, I'll invite Joan, too? What about next Friday night at around 7 p.m.?" Declan said. "Sure that works for me." Tyler replied with a grin as he thought to himself… and there it is, the invite I needed! He took the bait, hook line and sinker. Next Friday night this would all be over once and for all, finally all his hard work would pay off.

Later that night Declan was lying on the sofa next to Sarah while they watched a movie and thought he'd better tell her about having company. "Sarah, I invited Tyler over for dinner to meet Joan next Friday night at 7 p.m. Is that ok?" "Of course, what should I make? You guys eat together all the time what does Tyler like to eat?" "Let me fish around with him to see what he's in the mood for. We have a week no rush." "No rush? Only a man would say that to a woman. I have to call Joanie, go to the grocery store and look through my recipes, too. Maybe Joanie can whip up a cake. Then I have to clean the house and make sure everything is picked up after you. It's great that you thought of inviting Joanie so that Tyler won't be the third wheel!" "Yes, I was surprised he agreed he usually hates when I try to set him up. Sarah love, don't meddle, he's coming to discuss my bachelor party so don't push them together. Let's just see what happens. They may hate each other." "Bachelor Party, really, when were you going to tell me that you were having one? I assumed you weren't having one." "Now, love you're having a bachelorette party aren't you?" "Yes" she giggled "but that's different no naked woman is jumping out of a cake." "No naked women are jumping out of any cake for me either. I swear it's going to be just the guys playing pool at Casey's and having a few beers. No women at all." "Yeah, if half of what you said about Tyler is true, at least one naked woman is happening."

Tyler and Declan worked the night shift on Monday and were cooking burgers in the kitchen when the alarm sounded. Shutting the stove off, both men ran to jump into gear. Leaping onto the truck they heard Chief Ryan say, "Men, we received a call about a fire at 123 Elm Street, be ready; seems the entire house is in flames." "Yes, sir!" all the team responded. When they pulled up to the street the smoke and flames were raging through the roof. As a woman came running towards them she shouted, "Help us, my father is still inside...we couldn't get him out." She said with tears streaming down her face while she coughed and choked on her words. "Miss calm down, you say your father is inside what about your mother?"

"No, we are both safe …but my father, please, please save him. I think he fell asleep next to the electric space heater. I told him they were dangerous but he never listened." "Ok, move over to the side and out of the way of danger and let us take it from here." "Men, there's an elderly man still trapped inside. Declan and Tyler, Paul and Colin; work together!" Chief Ryan exclaimed. "Yes, Chief!" all four men said in unison. Declan and Tyler worked their way to the living room through the fog of smoke while Paul and Colin worked the hoses trying to put the fire out as they went. They reached the elderly man at the same time. His lifeless body was face down on the floor. As Paul and Colin picked him up to carry him out the ceiling began to give way. The beam started to crack but before it fell on Declan's head Tyler jumped and pushed him out of the way. Both men sighed in relief. "Now. let's get the hell out of here." The man was immediately given oxygen and already in an ambulance with his wife and daughter for further evaluation.

After the fire was out, and under control, except for the smoldering embers, Declan walked over to Tyler and patted him on the back. "Tyler, great teamwork in there today you saved my ass." "I'm just doing my job Lt. Foley, just doing my job." "Hey, about Friday night, what should we have? Sarah is open to suggestions and I don't think Joan will mind if you choose for all of us." "What about that 5 layer Mexican dip she makes? We could use it for a taco base. YUM, tacos sounds great! Haven't been in the mood lately so this would be a real treat." "Great, tacos it is. I'll let her know tonight."

Later that night lying in bed Declan remembered his conversation with Tyler. "Sarah, I talked to Tyler today about food and he suggested tacos with your Mexican dip that you love to make." "Now you tell me, it's already Tuesday. I swear Declan if I didn't love you so much I would strangle you." Sarah said as she wrapped her hands around his throat. "Why, what did I do?" he said as he made fake choking sounds. "Only that the recipe calls for all the ingredients that I don't have. At least I know Joanie likes tacos, too. I'm going to have to stop at the store before coming home to cook that night. I have a busy next few days with night classes at the shop and won't be able to go to the store until Friday. That's all." "Tell me what you need, you can make me a list and I can go shopping." "Are you kidding me, you shop and with a list? I don't think so. The last time I sent you to the store you came back with beer and chips. No, I will go on my way home Friday. You guys will have to talk while I cook." Sarah exclaimed.

She started to make a mental list in her head

as Declan grabbed her and pulled her against him. "That's one of the reasons I love you so much. You know me too well." "Yes, I do. I know everything about you. Even where you're ticklish." She squealed with laughter as she jumped on top of him and started to tickle him. They ended up on the floor laughing and kissing. They both lay on their backs and looked at each other as Sarah whispered, "Make love to me, Declan make me feel like a teenager again. Promise me even when we're an old married couple we'll still do this; we'll still feel like this." "I promise love, I will always want you like this until death us do part and even after that. I love you too much to ever want to stop. I only hope you feel the same about me when we're an old married couple." "I promise to love you forever." She said as they made love.

Tyler was sure he had his plan set down to the last second. It seemed like the longest week of his life. Friday was finally here and tonight was the night. All of his efforts would pay off. Acting very cool he smiled as Declan walked into the firehouse. "Hey man, all set for tonight? I've been thinking about Sarah's tacos and dip all week." "Hey Tyler, yes all set. Sarah's stopping at the store on her way home from work. We can watch something while we wait. I just got a new 60-inch TV with all the premium channels. There has to be a game on and I'm sure the girls won't mind." I said to Tyler. "Sounds great, just don't get yourself killed on the job today or I'll have to go without you." Tyler replied. I laughed and said, "You wish! Sarah is all mine and I don't share or play well with others who try to take what's mine." "I hear you, just kidding." Tyler said with a laugh. Little does he know I wouldn't want Sarah if she were the last woman on earth.

Thankfully, the day went off without a hitch. Just a few minor fires nothing serious. At 5:00 the two men grabbed their coats and went to Sarah's house.

Sarah went to 3 different stores looking for the ground cumin she needed forth dip. I can't believe this; don't big grocery stores carry all the spices you need? What the hell is going on? First, Joanie has an emergency and cancels now I don't have dessert and now this. I'm in spice hell. It's because I'm in a hurry that's it. Now what else do I need, refried black beans, chili powder, sour cream, shredded cheddar cheese, black olives, tomatoes and green onions. Don't forget hamburger meat and tortilla chips she reminded herself. As she walked through the store she stopped and said "lettuce" and looked around to make sure no one heard that. She walked to the register and loaded her items on the counter. As the clerk started ringing up the items she began to get a shiver that ran up the length of her arm and made the hairs stand on end. She thought to herself, what the hell was that?

Declan and Tyler walked into the living room and Tyler gasped at the TV. "Wow, you got this for her place what did you get for yours?" "I just bought this one since after the wedding we'll be living here. I'm giving up my place. This one is closer to both our jobs and much bigger." "Talking about the wedding, I was thinking about a game for the bachelor party. My sister's friend was telling me about one the other night. Here, sit in this chair. Come on Declan, work with me, let me show you how it goes." "OK, but if you get freaky- I'll have to kill you." Declan said with a frown. "Sit, don't be a frigging baby. Now I'll have to blindfold you and tie you to the chair, hands and feet." Tyler said. "Now wait a minute, don't go 50 shades on me." Declan yelled. Tyler just gave me a smirk and said, "Oh my God, Declan, stop being a pussy, shut up and sit down." It felt like something just didn't seem right, but he mentally brushed it away and sat in the chair. "Ok, now what?" Tyler began to tie his feet together; he tied Declan's arms behind his back and added the finishing touch... a blindfold. With a whoosh of his hands and a spin around the chair Tyler transformed into his true self, Joseph Riley Griffin.

As he began to chant he pulled the blindfold down. Declan was dumbfounded with disbelief. "Joseph, Joseph Griffin is it really you, brother? How is this possible? It can't be you. This is some sort of trickery. Who are you?" "Yes, it's me Joseph, but you're no brother of mine. Finally, the day has come for me to exact my revenge!" he smiled. "REVENGE?" Declan couldn't believe his eyes or his ears as he sat helplessly tied to the chair with all of his powers rendered useless.

13

<u>Final Showdown</u>

As Sarah started up the steps to the apartment she heard voices. It sounds like Declan is arguing with someone, it can't be Tyler, she thought. That can't be, they never fight, they kid around and wrestle but this doesn't sound like they're kidding. Tyler's going to be our Best Man.... what could they be fighting about? Before she could reach for the knob, Sarah notices that it's open slightly, luckily for her they don't hear her coming. They are in the living room. As Sarah slides into the kitchen undetected she thinks to herself, I hate spying on them but I better see what's going on before I stop them, she decides. Could it be someone else they invited over? It can't be Tyler talking; this voice has an Irish accent. Peering around the corner she sees a man much taller and slimmer than Tyler. No, it's not Tyler, she realizes, this man has red hair. She's positive it's someone she's never met but as she sees the back of him shivers run through her body as she starts to think he looks and sounds so familiar. Where do I know him from? OH MY GOD it's a burglar and she spots Declan tied to a chair. What do I do? Call the Police, no he might kill him. And, where's Tyler – is he already dead? Oh no, think Sarah think you can do this you can save the man you love. Only the Prince comes to the rescue in fairy tales this is real life and I would die if anything happened to him. I don't think I could go on without him, I love him so desperately, You're a Guilford girl do something! She began to really listen to the conversation now hoping and waiting for a chance to be able to do something but instead what she hears makes her feel like she's in some kind of weird nightmare, it can't be real. It's not possible, who the Hell is Mary? Is this over another woman? Is Declan seeing someone else, NO this is ridiculous, I know he loves me.

Riley starts to taunt Declan. "Finally, the day has come for my revenge! I've waited centuries for this day. Since the day you ruined my family. Your damn curse killed Mary and I both on the same day. Any idea as to what that did to our parents? NO? No, because you left and never looked back you didn't give a shit. All you ever cared about was, Declan. I checked on my parents when I got my memories back the first time. Did you know they both died less than a year after us? My poor mother died of a broken heart from the stress and my father a heart attack, he couldn't take another loss. So this time I thought how can I get that close to him? Tyler was a clever ruse, no? You never saw me coming." "It's not over yet Joseph!" "I prefer

Riley now; I decided to keep using my middle name. You can handle that right Declan? You're used to calling Mary different names. Let me see there was Mary my sister first." Sarah held in a gasp. "Then Maggie, Nora, Ann, Catherine and now Sarah. You see Declan my old friend I've been at the center of all her lives too. When you cast your stupid spell you made mistake, you didn't think about what would happen to her twin now did you? I've paid the price for that for all these centuries. At first I didn't know if she was in on it, my dear sweet innocent Mary, but realized when I talked to her when she was Maggie she didn't have a clue." I started to fume, "What! You talked to Maggie? Why, how could you? Who the hell is Nora?" I said as my temper began to rise. Riley continued, "Due time brother, due time, this is my time not yours, just shut up and listen."

As he waved his arm, thick, black tape covered my mouth. He continued again; "I'll give you a chance to speak when I feel I need a response. I want you to have the whole story before I kill you. You see I was reborn too but I somehow kept the knowledge with me, things got weird at 16 but only on my 18th birthday, did it all come flooding back to me. Maggie was an experiment you see; I was Raymond Bennett the man who accused her of being a witch. Oh, yes, at first I thought to myself how could I do this to my own sister but she started it all when she fell in love with you. She used to come to me to talk about everything until you. Didn't you wonder why I dropped dead minutes after her?" Riley said dryly gesturing to Declan and removing the tape. "No, I thought you had a heart attack when you realized I was a warlock." Warlock, Sarah heard, no this can't be true she thought as she blinked her eyes open and shut several times, you're hearing things because of the adrenaline rush going through your mind. Sarah had her hands over her ears and through her hair in nervous gestures as if trying to block and brush away all that was happening. There's no such thing as witches and warlocks...is this some kind of sick game they're playing? Is it code for something else? As Riley gestured a wave of the hand, WHOOSH the tape went back across Declan's mouth. "Don't get any ideas of using your magic Declan I can feel you trying but I have a binding spell on you. I don't really need the ropes or tape to keep you seated but I like how it looks, seeing you bound and gagged, gives me great pleasure." He said with a laugh.

"You see, you missed one of Mary's rebirths. She was born in 1750 as Nora Murphy; I knew I had to do something before you found her. I went in search of a witch. I found Delilah O'Shea and I killed her, sliced her head off before she realized what was happening. Ah, you recognize the name. She was a witch more powerful than you or your family and I've inherited her powers. Dumb bitch even let me have a golden sword for protection. What? What's that? I can't hear you, want to say something?" WHOOSH Riley waved his hand. "OUCH! Oh for Christ sake, stop that! What the bloody hell are you talking about? There was no Nora and the Council would never have allowed that, they would have killed you before you could talk." I shouted. "I'm not as stupid as you think dear Declan; I devised a plan, brilliant even. I carried it out very well if I do say so myself. It was self- defense and you know the council won't punish for that." "Great, because brother, it's going to be self-defense when I slice your fucking lying head off." I could feel my eyes began to flame. "Calm yourself your powers will not have any effect on me. Now where was I? Ah yes, I even had a council member front and center when it happened; he saw the whole thing.

After I gained my powers and assumed that I would now be immortal I found Mary who was now Nora Murphy and I drowned the bitch. You see, with each and every new life I had, the more I detested her. If she could have just listened to me that night, this would have never happened. Of course, we'd both be dead but that's life. But like clockwork, I dropped dead within 10 minutes of her death. Talk about a pain in the ass. At least this time at 16 not only did my memories come back so did the power; too bad for you but wonderful for me. At least the next time I'd still be powerful." He said with a laugh.

"Then there was Ann, you're going to love this, it was *really* good, wait for it, I was Andrew her twin, talk about irony. Didn't it seem odd when we turned 18 how I made our parents send me away to school? I couldn't stand the sight of the two of you. However, I did come back before the blessed event. I didn't want you to have a spawn so I had to kill her before she gave birth. So I transformed myself into the doctor. That's why I had to get out of the house right away so that I could die yet again. Oh, Declan, you have been such a pain in my ass. Getting impatient? I'm almost done; let's see, on to Catherine." I can't believe what I'm hearing. How did I miss this so many times what a bloody idiot I've been! Was I so blinded by love that I never saw what was right there in front of me? I have to get out of this before he kills Sarah she'll be home soon. Sarah standing in the doorway in shock continued to listen as the tears began to roll down her face.

"Catherine, yes, in that life I actually was born Wayne Lye and at 18 it happened again, but this time I waited because I needed to figure out what I was doing wrong. In this life I became a real doctor." He smiled at Declan. "DR. LYE! You killed Catherine and our child too?" "Now you're following the pattern, good job!"

"Yes, you see as luck would have it, I was in the ER that night when you came in. Even though I wasn't quite ready, I decided what the hell is one more life; but just one." He continued, "I was so sick to death of the two of you by now. I wasn't born Tyler Vega in this life but cloaked myself to get close to you. You see I figured all the other times I had gotten close to Mary didn't work. This time I'd try getting close to you. You never saw me coming. I played the devoted best friend and choked on every word, every damn last word. But I knew I had to kill you first to break the spell and then and only then - I could live for eternity. The night we rescued Sarah from the store fire, I knew we'd found Mary; again at last. Funny how every time she has those green eyes, isn't it? Yes, I noticed too." Sarah stood in shocked silence and with the realization settling in at that moment, she realized that all of her phobias were just flashes of her past lives. Ways that she had died at the hands of her own twin brother, a twin she never knew existed. She'd always thought reincarnation was possible but hearing it really was just a bit overwhelming. Knowing that no matter what she cannot let Declan die, she can't watch as he kills Declan. He may be my brother but I have no memories or feelings for him. Think, think Sarah, she ordered herself, what did he say about killing that witch Delia or something? Yes, yes he chopped her head off with a golden sword. Oh no, there has to be another way, I can't do that. I just can't, can I?

"If you touch one hair on her head, I'll kill you, you bastard." I said in a tone that made Riley laugh out loud. "Seriously, you still think you can beat me? That's not going to happen this time. I have this final round, your powers are bound, and you're helpless until you take your last breath. I am going to slice your head right off your bloody shoulders. I'm going to take my time, inch by inch, cut by cut. I'll take away your voice and watch you suffer. You'll suffer for all of them, all of the Mary's and the Riley's that you destroyed. I'll watch you bleed and bleed and scream with no sound. I'll look into your fire eyes and I'll laugh with Victory as your fucking head drops to the ground and rolls away. I may shrink it and keep it as a memento, maybe put it on a chain and wear it around my neck. Then and only then will vengeance be mine! Not to mention, I'll have your powers as well. You'll be dead and the curse will be broken at long last and this time when Mary dies she'll stay dead and I'll live forever with unimaginable powers! What now? Interrupting again? Oh go ahead but make it quick I'm getting bored."

"There's just one little flaw in your insane plan." I said angrily. "What about the council? They'll hunt you down like the bastard you are and then you'll feel what torture really is. They won't just slice your head off. They'll make you wish you'd never been born or should I say, reborn? Even if I die, at least I know Mary and I will be together forever in the heavenly afterlife; while you rot in eternity in the fiery, rotten stenches of Hell."

"Declan my boy, wrong again. You see I checked with a dear close friend that I have on the council. In case you didn't know, the council recently went through let's say an overhaul. I now have friends on the council and they said it's well within my rights to kill you. After all you've killed me too many times to count and never paid for it. Mary and I never asked to be reborn. You were playing God again even way back then just like you do now. I'm just stopping the vicious cycle you began all those centuries ago. And Mary is just a big fat bonus she's not a witch so she doesn't count to them. I could let her live and erase her memories of you. Let her die on her own, have a normal life, but then what punishment would you really get. I not really happy about killing her, it's just that I know how much it will hurt you. I hope she comes home soon. I've dragged this on far too long now. My first thought was to kill her first and make you watch and then have some fun with you. But then again, I'd die, you'd live and she'd just be reborn. Since that's not going to happen I'll just have to start with you. Can't you see it Declan? Just image your head rolling down the hall and stopping at her feet, maybe she'll have a heart attack and I won't have to kill her, no, I won't let that happen. I want her to know that you killed her, that you are the reason for everything bad in all our lives. You did this to us all. You cursed our family you destroyed all of our lives. Our parents never recovered. You've destroyed the Griffin family for the last time and I'm so going to relish in the victory of your death."

I began to think… let me try another approach, as I kept my voice calm though I really wanted to scream out to protect Sarah and Joan from walking into this, since Riley this maniac has my powers bound, I can't feel where Sarah was as I normally can. "Joseph, I mean Riley, what the hell happened to you? You loved Mary why would you want to end her life. I understand why you want me dead and the other Mary's you knew would be reborn, but you know Sarah won't. She is your kin; she is your blood. You know if I die before her, she won't be reborn again." "Do you think me the fool Declan? I tried to reason with Mary the day she ran off with you. I told her it was a big mistake that you weren't good enough for her. She told me that I was wrong, that I was jealous that she was happy, but that she'd wait awhile to decide and then she ran off to be with you that very night. I am her other half we shared the same womb for 9 months and still she chose you over me." "ENOUGH LET'S GET ON WITH IT!" Riley began to shout and conjured a long golden sword in his hands. "You see; I don't need all of your stupid incantations. I have more power than you know and soon I will have more."

Sarah thought to herself it's now or never, don't think just do. Riley was too busy screaming at Declan and walking towards him, that he didn't hear Sarah as she crept into the room. Before he could take another step she kicked the back of his knees with everything she had in her. With all of the love for Declan in her heart she grabbed the sword as he went down. As Riley jumped to his feet, his eyes met Sarah's and as in slow motion he relived the last moments he shared with Mary, his Sister his twin. No he could never hurt her, not Mary, let this be done he thought as Sarah turned with a sharp swift move and sliced off his head, as Riley's head rolled across the floor the spell on Declan was released. As I raced to her side screaming "NO!!!!!!!" Sarah dropped the sword and fell to her knees sobbing. I began to tell her she'll die in 10 minutes if what Riley said was true or the council would come. She couldn't hear me, the blood was rushing through her head, her ears were ringing and she felt like she was floating out of her body with all the adrenaline rushing through her veins. As I cradled my bloodied Sarah in my arms, I thought to myself, you have to help her, God, help me think please.

Suddenly Sarah started to feel strange but in a good way she began to feel the power that Riley held as it surged through her body from her head down to her toes and realized in an instant that she wasn't dying she was alive and living like never before! She smiled at me and said "I remember everything, all of it, all of my lives" she cried out. "Declan oh my love I remember all of it." As the relief began to wash over me, "You must have absorbed his powers and broke the curse when you killed him and by doing so, you ended the cycle. Because you are a more powerful Witch than I am now, my spell was broken too." "Mary oh Mary is it truly you?" Yes, it's me, Declan, I've missed you my love." With a wave of my hand and the fire in my eyes I sent Riley's body away in a flash. "Don't worry I sent him home to Ireland where he can finally be at peace with your parents." "I know this has been a shock for you but I've waited for centuries for this to happen one day but never really believed it would or could happen." As I get down on one knee and hold out my left hand with a wave of my right a black ring box appears. "Mary my love, I told you we'd be together forever and now we can, now that you are immortal too. Marry me, let's fly to wherever your heart desires I can't wait to be married, today Mary, let's start eternity." Yes, Declan Patrick Foley I will marry you. But there is a catch, can you call me Sarah? I feel funny even with all of my new or should I say old memories being called Mary as I was only Mary for such a short time." She smiles looking down as he places the ring on her finger. "But before you really commit to me, Sarah, I have to tell you something that I did. I tricked you at the astrological fair. I fixed the deck. And I may have listened in on a few of your private conversations on how to win your heart. I need you to know I don't want there to be secrets between us." She tried to suppress a smile, "Well in full disclose, I lied to you too. I was a virgin the night we made love for the first time. I wanted you so badly Declan and I knew what a gentleman you were, I figured you might say you couldn't steal my virtue or that we had to be married first so I lied about the boyfriend in college. There's never been anyone but you, only you Declan, you have always owned my body, mind and soul my heart has always been only for you." I pulled her close and softly kissed her lips. "My Love, I forgive you because I know how much my life sucks without you." "My heart has only belonged to you too. I've been holding onto something for you that I won't need any longer." I reached into my pocket and pulled out the locket.

"Do you remember the night I gave it to you?"
"My locket! I remember the night you gave it to
me." Sarah cried. "I took it the night you first died
and have carried through the centuries I spelled it
to locate you each time. It's how I was able to
always find you. But your gorgeous green eyes
were always the giveaway. I knew each time I
looked into them and fell in love every time I saw
them. It truly was love at first sight each and every
time. But this time we'll have the happily ever
after. I love you so much Sarah." Smiling, Sarah
only replied, "I love you more."

While the happy couple celebrated their love,
their engagement, a woman sitting all alone in a
castle in France watched through her crystal ball.
She sat with her long black hair in a purple gown.
She wore purple ribbons in her hair, a silver locket
around her neck and a diamond ring and silver
wedding band on her left ring finger. Rena Helena
watched in horror and shock, the love of her life

Riley Griffin as he took his last breath and die by the golden sword in the hands of Sarah Spencer. As they celebrated, the fury and rage inside her started to build as tears streaming down her face she began to curse.

She stood tossing the table and crystal ball. She was noticeably very pregnant. The baby inside her began to kick. "Hush little one, it's alright, Mommy will make this all better. Don't you worry little Riley; Mommy will make them both pay for what they did to your Father. You'll have to grow up without knowing him - but make no mistake, Mommy will take care of them as soon as you're born," she murmured softly to her unborn baby.

THE END

Made in United States
North Haven, CT
14 April 2023